50p

D1356494

THE COLOUR OF DARKNESS

Also by Alan Dipper

THE WAVE HANGS DARK
THE HARD TRIP
THE GOLDEN VIRGIN

ALAN DIPPER

The Colour of
Darkness

London
MICHAEL JOSEPH

First published in Great Britain by Michael Joseph Ltd
52 Bedford Square, London, W.C.1
1974

© 1974 by Alan Dipper

All Rights Reserved. No part of this publication
may be recorded, stored in a retrieval system,
or transmitted, in any form or by any means,
electronic, mechanical, photocopying, recording
or otherwise, without the prior permission
of the Copyright owner

ISBN 0 7181 1211 3

Set and printed in Great Britain by
Northumberland Press Limited, Gateshead,
in Granjon twelve on fourteen point
and bound by James Burn, Esher, Surrey

One for Giles

'You are blind? Consider then the Colour of Darkness . . .'

CHAPTER ONE

I stared blankly through the half-opened window. From the terrace below silver needles of rain leapt skyward like a faquir's bed of nails. I wondered at the perversity of my mind—why an Indian simile? It had rained continuously now for four days and I felt damp to the marrow; the cold weight of a wet world pressing scabs of blue mould into my mind.

The steady beat of the typewriter behind me hesitated, then stopped with an expensive and very final clatter, and Victoria said nervously, 'I'm sorry, sir, I did send a memo to the maintenance people last week.'

She was a sensitive girl, totally unfitted to deal with my sardonic brand of irritability. I walked over to her desk, pulled the paper from the machine, and said, 'Go on home. Have an early night for once—I'll finish it myself.'

I couldn't have surprised her more if I'd flung her over the desk and raped her. In the ten years she had worked for me, I don't suppose I had once showed that I noticed her as a human being. She had the face of a very intelligent and handsome blonde monkey; and a simian passion for collecting small objects. Her desk was a reflection of her mind, cluttered with trivia. She swept a small sea of ambiguous debris into a drawer, gulped, 'Yes, Minister,' and scuttled out of the room.

I walked back to the window holding the letter and read it very carefully through twice, then let it slip out

Ref 871/T/AFC

From: Origin:
Tomas Eliot Traherne   Ministry of Home Production
Member, Lavender Hill East

Report to Chairman of Subcommittee – Illegal Immigration

Note: copy to Chief Detective Inspector Lettcombe, New
       Scotland Yard

       Having regard to the increase of illegal entry to this
country, I bring the following facts to the notice of the
Committee:

       On 14th June 1974 I interviewed a young Indian woman, a
sister of the former ruler of Larishnapur (now Chumbari District)
in northern India:

Lakshmi Vasantasena

Date of birth, December 1954 (exact date not known)

Place of birth, Kandhla, Republic of India

Address, 109 Eaton Square, London SW1

Occupation, voluntary welfare worker and liaison officer to
  Race Relations Board (SW district)

Work permit no. 803/684/PD 108

Note: permission granted for indefinite domicile in United
       Kingdom
                                                        cont:

through the open sash. The rain took it, beat it to a pulp
and swilled the sodden scrap through a gutter into the
swollen Thames. I shut my eyes and the words seemed
still printed on the retinas. It was exactly three weeks
since Vashni had walked into this room.

I had not wished to see her. My appointment as Minister
of Home Production was six months old, and I was still
savouring the uncluttered air at the top of the power
tree. As I climbed, I built a labyrinth of protective devices
beneath. Not for me the easy bonhomie of the popular

politician; the possessor of real power should exist in astringent isolation. I needed two more years to tie up my own Party and my outside backers, then I would teach them all the tariff for riding tigers.

It was not easy to get in to see me.

Victoria had handed me the letter a week before and the first thing I noticed was a Welsh language overprint on the envelope. My attitude to the Land of my Fathers was decidedly ambivalent. I came up from the Valleys the hard way and I didn't care for reminders of my past. Not that we lived in poverty; God knows the Welsh have had a bellyful of that, but a war and a demanding peace brought more money to Brynmawr than had been seen since Offa the Dyke did his bit of building. Reared in the virtually classless society of Wales, how should I feel shame at my beginnings? Yet if not shame, what was it?

Since I left Oxford, pitchforked inevitably into politics by my need for power, I had been back only twice. Once to bury my mother in the raw rain and stark rites of a mountain Bethesda chapel; and again to hear a smooth eulogy droned for my father and a score of others in the great echoing foundry where he had spent his working life. I left on the next train. There was nothing to bury here but cold memories of a religious-minded giant, and no use now for a back that could support six men; or bare hands to bend a horseshoe straight. Not under a hundred tons of half-cooled iron. Ashes to ashes, slag to slag. When the Steel Corporation offered me compensation for his death, I was already adopted candidate for Lavender Hill East and my donation of it to the workers'

9

welfare fund won me a valuable paragraph in the national press ...

Even I could not fob off the writer of that letter with a few minutes' banality in the office of a permanent secretary. Her introduction was from as near Royalty as protocol would permit, and she asked for 'Advice on a problem concerning one of my countrymen'.

My constituency is a magnet pulling the adventurous and plain hungry from the worn out soil of the sub-continent. One in five of my people range from the jet of Bengal to pale ivory of the northern provinces—and I felt a physical revulsion at being near any of them. I don't know what shibboleth of the English middle classes I had absorbed to create such a phobia. Perhaps, when I made myself over in the image of a gin-and-tonic-belt Englishman, some trauma from the British Raj sank into my subconscious—or maybe my mother was frightened by a Swansea Lascar: 'There's funny now, Mrs Traherne love, a black man looking through the window ...'

I had the letter in my hand when Victoria announced my visitor and tactfully scuttled back to her room. I prefer my dingy office in the Commons to the gleaming glass and steel of the Ministry building, and I conduct most of my business here. My desk is gigantic. A perfect piece of lifemanship, emphasizing the distance between the Great Man and his privileged visitors; but, even with the river to reflect it, the light is bad and at first I could see little but a shadowy female shape.

When meeting someone for the first time I like to remain silent until, from sheer nervousness, they speak.

It gives me an instant advantage. However, this woman had a most disconcerting self-possession. I rose, switched on the desk light, and waved my hand at the chair opposite. She sat gracefully and faced me, hands folded, face utterly calm. She sat with a stillness I had not thought possible. With a firmness that suggested she was part of the chair—part of the very earth on which the building rested. I could not even detect her breathing, yet I knew I was with the most vitally alive woman I had ever seen. I lowered myself into my chair and forced my voice to the proper bureaucratic pitch.

'Miss—ah—Vasantasena?'

She smiled; a flash of light in the pale oval face. I could not speak again. Her eyes were huge, the iris so dark that the white showed blue. At the nape of her neck a carved silver circle caught back the long black hair. There was an overall effect of slimness, but, under the white silk of her blouse, the shoulders were wide and strong, tapering to a silver belt at her waist that looked hardly larger than that which held her hair. I looked away.

Where sex was concerned I had led, for these days, an austere life. I had known, both intellectually and intuitively, that the power I craved would not survive surrender to a woman. I had a few affairs—safe, well managed liaisons, little more than sops to the huge body I inhabit—but I never lost control of any such situation. I could, even while performing, detach my mind from the act and observe the absurdities of the basic rite.

The woman said, 'Lakshmi Vasantasena will do,

Minister. My full name is ridiculously long. It is good of you to see me.'

Her voice was low pitched, yet I could have heard her at the other end of that long dark room; it had the carrying power of birdsong. There was no trace of accent. She paused, then went on, 'Minister, I work as you know, for Race Relations.' I nodded; she hesitated again, then, 'A man has vanished ...'

I started to speak, 'The police ...'

She waved a slim hand impatiently. It was a totally unselfconscious gesture, but I realized with a pang, that it held a sureness of authority I could never know however high I climbed.

She went on as though I had not spoken, 'I have a servant—a daughter of my old ayah. Six months ago her son started out to come to this country. He wrote to her just as he was leaving; she has proof he left India. He is an active, healthy young man—and he has vanished.'

Her hands were folded now in her lap. Her spine was straight, not touching the back of the chair, yet she was completely relaxed. I was reminded of my cat; I have always admired the economy of effort in felines. A muscle is moved, the required movement is accomplished, utter relaxation follows. A human being, in comparison, has perpetual St Vitus's dance.

I spoke into the intercom, 'Victoria, get Home Office —Immigration. Check on an Indian national: male, young, approximate date of entry, January this year.'

I turned to the woman, 'What's the man's name?'

She hesitated very slightly, 'Chota Dal. The Chota part is more of a nickname—it means small.'

'Any other means of identifying him?'

'Not really. I was very young and I can only just remember him but it seems to me that he wasn't a very nice little boy. He used to—cringe.' She paused, then went on thoughtfully, 'But being of sweeper caste is not very nice even in modern India. I'm afraid I don't remember being kind to him but Larri, my brother, would have seen he wasn't made too miserable; there were over three hundred servants in the old palace and he knew every one of them. Of course I was only about nine at that time and my brother sent me over here to school when I was ten.'

The line was still open. I said, 'Victoria, did you get that?' Her voice crackled through the receiver, 'Yes, sir, I already have the department.'

I snapped off the switch. 'If he got here,' I said, 'they'll tell us.'

The woman opposite me moved uneasily; the marvellous poise was flawed.

'Mr Traherne,' she said, 'I most certainly did not intend to deceive you but ...' She hesitated for the briefest moment. 'This man could have entered the country illegally.'

I took a deep breath and stood up. I was bewilderingly conscious that in the few minutes we had passed together, this woman had affected me more than anyone I had met in my thirty-five years, yet anger burned deep down in my guts. I hated to be tricked—particularly by her.

'With that introduction,' I said coldly, 'you were sure of getting to see me. However, I can do nothing for you but advise contacting the police. I shall, of course, report it myself otherwise I should be compounding a felony.'

She rose and faced me. In the light of the lamp I could now see her very clearly. I had been deceived by her apparent frailty. Her breasts were large, moving freely under the taut silk blouse. She followed the prevailing fashion, and the delicate outlines were not blurred by any support. From the tiny waist the hips flared and tapered to legs fine boned as a thoroughbred racehorse. She turned towards the door, and the smartly cut linen skirt seemed very full of her. I had seen such figures before, naked on a stone frieze at an exhibition of Indian temple carvings—beautifully, unequivocally female.

She was not used to being dismissed; not even by Her Majesty's Ministers. Her voice was equally cold. 'Thank you, Mr Traherne,' she said precisely. 'It was kind of you to waste your time on me.'

I have not got where I am by letting even my own considerable pride stand in my way. If I want something enough, I have the power to ignore, not only the outside world, but my whole inner being except that desire. Now, strange as it seemed, I had not the slightest doubt that this woman was to be very much part of my life. As I opened the door my arm brushed her breast. In such accidental contacts there can be more excitement than in the full sex act, yet my pulse remained steady. There was no shock; just a feeling of warm familiarity.

She said, 'Thank you,' and smiled, and it was not the smile of one stranger for another, nor even the subtle female expression of promise for a possible lover, but a friend for a friend in the shared intimacy of years of living. Without thought I slipped my arm through hers and led her downstairs.

An enormous blue Bentley was waiting in the court-yard. A uniformed Indian chauffeur handed her in, and I wondered idly how she had managed to fix his work permit. She wound the window down and said, 'My brother and I will be at your meeting tonight. Do you think you could warn them about coming here illegally? It really does lead to appalling misery. I will see you afterwards.' It was a statement as inevitable and casual as a wife saying she would meet her husband after work.

Victoria had arranged that I address my coloured con-stituents that evening. I had been criticized, justly enough, for neglecting their interests. This meeting was to put that right, but I had agreed to it only on condition it was held immediately before my vacation. I was to leave the following morning for a month of idleness in the sun; only Victoria knew where I was going, and I had promised to roast her over a slow fire of red tape if she let anyone but the P.M. himself know where I was. I would not, therefore, be caught up in the endless proliferation of arguments and media interviews inevitable after such a conference.

My constituency may not be the most glamorous of territories but I still like to look at it whenever possible. Its people put me on the political map, and I'm decently grateful, but I'd had a long, hard day terminating in the time-bomb of Miss Lakshmi Vasantasena. I was still worried about that little surprise packet; I would be see-ing it again very soon and I was quite prepared for it to blow up in my face. I explained carefully to myself that she was just another coffee-coloured headache, that I was on my way to meet two thousand more, and that I disliked the lot of them; but we had crossed the river and my driver was ferreting his way through the rabbit-maze of riverside Battersea before I could close my eyes and unreel a holiday film of hot beaches and deep blue sea in the cinema of my skull.

I was half asleep when the lorry hit us. I heard my driver shout, 'Christ!' And I was staring stupidly at a mess of tangled metal that a second before had been the front end of an elegant official Daimler. As the remnant of the car spun in slow circles on the greasy tarmac, I could see the driver's arms protruding from a flattened chaos of engine and upholstery. The effect was of an obscene piece of modern sculpture. I leaned forward, saw half a dead face glaring at me from near road level, and vomited. One part of my mind noted that I had retained the habits of an English gentleman and used the open window beside me—'Good for you, Tomas bach; clean that is!'

The Daimler slid gently to a stop in a warehouse gate-way, and the trapped arms jerked forward in a cheerful beckoning motion. I couldn't bring myself to slide past them, and scrabbled frantically at the nearside door. It opened smoothly and I stepped out into the rain.

Apart from a slight cut on my right cheekbone, I was completely unhurt, and, as soon as I established my identity, the police slapped on a plaster, tucked me into a patrol car and were all for taking me to hospital. I knew that if I started thinking about those arms I was in trouble, so I told them to drive me to the meeting. There was nothing I could do for my driver. The lorry, an eight-ton gravel truck, was abandoned fifty yards down the street. The driver had panicked and run.

I made a good speech. It wasn't the one I had prepared —that was good, too, in its way and followed the golden rule; there wasn't a concrete fact or promise in it. A politician who commits himself in public should stick to parish councils. Nine-tenths of government is done by committee work and private meetings, and a Member who wastes important facts on the public creates alarm and despondency on both sides of the House. You can't run a country if people have endless opportunities of invoking democratic procedure; but on that night my training deserted me.

I had seen a man die. I didn't know him; he was just someone from the driving pool. If this had not happened I wouldn't have recognized him when next we met. While I sipped oversweet tea waiting for my hands to stop shaking, my attendant policeman filled me in on the man's background, as he'd picked it up from H.Q. over the car radio ...

Henry Nosworthy, forty-five years old, three children and a wife; semi-detached villa at Wimbledon; non-smoker; well known as a fine amateur musician. Now, eight tons of gravel travelling at fifty m.p.h. had changed all that. A ripple in an ocean of nearly four billion human beings had flattened out, but would that change the ocean? I walked on to the stage depressed and anxious, and went into the official routine; then I stopped. I got started again and drew to another halt when I saw Lakshmi's face in the front row. 'There's a good one,

Tomas, upset is it over a brown face?' I decided I must stop talking to myself in Welsh, then lifted my head and stared out over the dark sea of faces. A sea? A minuscule drop in a planet-drowning flood. A moving, rising, flood melting one drop to another, and how separate a drop from the ocean or the ocean from a drop?

The chairman murmured anxiously, 'Are you all right, Minister?'

I looked at my hands and they were still shaking, then saw again Lakshmi's calm face. The hall was strangely quiet. I lifted my head and said, 'A man has died tonight. An ordinary man, a white Englishman. I did not know him neither did you, yet he is your loss and mine ...'

I spoke for an hour. I have the speech because it was so widely reported, otherwise I should not have remembered a word. I am told it was the best speech of my life and 'had a profound influence on race relations throughout the country'. At one point I remembered Lakshmi's request and inveighed against the misery caused by illegal entry into the country. Against basic political instincts I gave them facts and figures and promises—I even brought in Lakshmi's missing man as an illustration.

When I stopped the applause nearly lifted the roof. The platform was suddenly full of black and brown figures, arguing, gesticulating, trying to shake my hand. The voices blended in a roar and the sea crashed in my head. I came to with my head in Lakshmi's lap. It seemed the right place for it. Warm, scented, and somehow familiar. I kept my eyes closed and made the best of it for a few minutes, while her hand stroked my hair. My mind had never been so active. There is no doubt that certain situations, certain stimuli, raise the consciousness as high above ordinary living level as waking is from sleep.

I opened my eyes and started to get up. A strong hand helped me and an amused voice said, lightly, 'Now don't disappoint me, Minister. What you have to say is 'Where am I?'

I straightened up and faced the voice. Its possessor had a charming face; one I had seen somewhere before. A face a few years younger than mine but with more wrinkles round the eyes—lines formed of laughter and an enormous tolerance of human frailty. A nose like a knife, wide generous mouth, and a chin almost feminine in its delicacy. A pale-brown face attached to a lean, tough body. The arm that supported me felt as though it could lift my hundred and ninety pounds clear of the ground. His smile was infectious; I said gravely, 'Where am I?' and found myself laughing with him.

'One step from a large drink,' he said. 'Dawa!'

A figure came forward with a tray. I sank getting on for half a tumbler of neat brandy and felt very much better.

Lakshmi said, 'Mr Tomas Eliot Traherne, Minister of Home Production—His Highness the twenty-third Rajah of Larishnapur, King of Jalindar, King of the Eight Hills, Shivaro, Lord of Vishnaoprag ...'

He said, 'Shut up, Vashni, or I'll bung this glass at you,' and held out a sinewy brown hand. I shook it and he went on, 'I must apologize for my sister, her sense of humour stuck in the lower fifth at Roedean. Please call me Larri—everyone else does.'

I have never encouraged the free use of forenames.

When I am in America I find it disconcerting to be introduced as 'Minister' and, five minutes later, called 'Tom', but the sense of intense familiarity that hung about Lakshmi enveloped Larishnapur also. It was like putting on an old and favourite suit, or meeting a schoolfriend after many years' absence.

I said, 'You have been most kind, Larri, and so has Miss Vasantasena.' She looked up at me, lips quivering with amusement.

'Surely I am to be included in this *entente cordiale*, Minister—my friends call me Vashni.'

It was then I noticed she was wearing a sari. A simple blue thing with a bird motif embroidered on the border, and, oddly enough, it made her look both younger and astonishingly mature. With the softening of that opulent curve of hips she could have been sixteen, but the strange face stared calmly at me, speaking for itself.

'All right,' it seemed to say, 'it could be that I am your woman, but try no tricks with me, my man, for I am a thousand years old.'

'I am most honoured,' I said uneasily, 'but I would not like you to think—particularly after the great kindness you and your brother have shown—I mean ...'

Larri put his palms together and bowed.

'It is always an honour to help a Sahib—Sahib.'

For a moment his gravity fooled me, then I laughed, grasped his hand, and said earnestly, 'Larri, for a native —you're a white man!'

'Dear God,' Vashni groaned, 'another clown! That's all I needed!'

After that the evening blurred a little. The chauffeur's

mangled form still lurked on the fringes of my mind, and I was grateful to join in the foolery of this enchanting pair. They swept me into a midnight-blue Bentley and fed me Scotch from a built-in bar that would have served any reasonably-sized hotel. Larri used a radio telephone to order dinner, and I sank back on the cushions and closed my eyes. Perhaps it was the mixture of drinks, but it seemed entirely natural that my free hand should be held cosily by Vashni against the warmth of her thigh.

Eaton Square is still a very desirable address, but some of the glories of the austere terraces have departed. It is not, for instance, usual to own an entire house. Larri, it appeared, to avoid feeling cramped, had bought leases on two and knocked them together.

Inside, the house was a strange mixture of exquisite western taste, with an eastern thread woven almost imperceptibly through the pattern. Dinner was entirely Western. I have, perhaps, a rather coarse palate and dislike elaborate food. Larri provided Dublin Bay prawns, a leg of mutton, and an excellent stilton. I would imagine the claret was something special, but I have never subscribed to the mystique of wine and was content, without comment, to help him through two bottles while his sister sipped a glass of water.

We ate in a pleasant panelled room overlooking the square. The table was small, but even so Vashni sat closer to me than was strictly necessary. From under slightly drooping lids little escaped Larishnapur's dark, amused eyes. At one point he said lazily, 'Vashni darling, if you actually *lean* on our guest he won't be able to devour my excellent Welsh sheep.'

She blushed and sat primly upright.

'That reminds me,' I said hastily; 'why Wales? Your letter came from there.' The letter seemed a long time ago.

Larri smiled, 'You wouldn't think it to look at us, but we work hard—at least I do.'

'Now look here ...' Vashni exploded.

He joined his hands in mockery, 'Well, she does do a bit, I suppose, but I, at least, need an escape route. We have a house in Wales—Pembroke actually. We're going down tomorrow; why don't you come?'

I looked at Vashni and said unhappily, 'I'd like nothing better, but I'm booked abroad for a month.'

Somehow the blue of West Indian seas seemed suddenly tawdry.

'How did you find it?' I asked absently.

'I didn't. The indispensable Dawa Chand bullied me into it.' Hearing his name the man appeared silently beside the table. Larri waved a hand and he vanished.

'Poor devil,' I said. 'What happened to his face?'

'We *do* work hard, you know,' Vashni's voice was serious. 'For once, Larri wasn't joking. We run a clinic for our people. You politicians have no conception of the problem; there are thousands of the very poor from all over India and Pakistan. Not poor as you understand poverty, but poor to the point of starvation. I often wonder how they got the money together to come here in the first place.'

'You know well enough,' Larri said grimly, 'but you won't let yourself believe it. There's a hire purchase system, particularly for the illegals; the money-lenders bleed them for the rest of their lives—and throw in a bit of blackmail as makeweight.'

Vashni looked distressed. 'Well anyway,' she said, 'when they get ill they daren't go to a doctor. Some of them can't get jobs and they starve ...' She looked fondly across the table. 'Larri spends half his income on them.'

'And you found Dawa Chand there?'

'No, I found him a few months ago. Someone had done a really artistic carving job on him. We patched him up and he wouldn't leave us. He's not exactly pretty, and he has eyes like a demented rabbit—but he's utterly devoted.'

'But Wales?' I asked. The thought of those two beautiful sophisticates against the rugged coast of Cymru seemed so incongruous.

'Dawa came off a ship at Pembroke Dock,' Vashni said. 'He was ill and some farmer took him back home and nursed him. He thinks Wales is Vishnu's seventh sphere.'

'He seems to be natural Samaritan fodder,' I said rather tartly.

Vashni went pale and moved away from me. 'I am afraid we cannot claim to be a Levitical nation, Minister,' she said.

An awkward silence was broken by Dawa Chand materializing out of the shadows. I felt a surge of pity as I looked at that ruined face, split and flattened by the scar into a curious resemblance to an animal's muzzle; but the effect was not at all sinister. I searched my mind for where I had seen him before—him or something like him—and, as he bent over Larri, I looked straight into his eyes. Frightened eyes, bulging with emotion at being so close to his idol, the divided nostrils twitching as he talked—and I had it. A film cartoon rabbit, a child's idea of a bunny, straight from the hand of Disney.

'What have you been up to, Minister?' Larri asked, 'Selling State secrets? A police inspector wants to talk to you.'

Dawa led me to a small room at the end of a corridor. I picked up the phone and it was oddly soft to my hand. A warm, brown, animal fur had been moulded round the instrument; and walls, ceiling, floor and furniture of the room were one smooth continuous sweep of the same pelts. It was like being inside an enormous Victorian hand muff, and the effect was extraordinarily soothing.

A voice called anxiously, 'Minister?'

'Yes, Traherne here.'

'Chief Inspector Lettcombe, sir, C.I.D. Sorry to disturb you, but I have a report on your accident.'

The evening up to now had been an enchantment. In the peace that pervaded this extraordinary house, the tight edges of my mind had uncurled. I realized I was happier than I had been for years. I wanted to fill my head with thoughts of Vashni. Now, abruptly, the chauffeur's arms waved through the broken spell.

I said coldly, 'Yes, Inspector?'

In the receiver the tinny voice sounded oddly embarrassed, 'Well, sir, I've just got this from one of the men on the Battersea manor, he picked it up from his snout—er—informer. We know who was driving the lorry ...'

'Well, arrest the damn fool,' I said impatiently, 'and charge him. That poor devil of a driver didn't have a chance. It's a clear case of manslaughter.'

There was a long pause, then: 'No, sir, he was after you. He had five hundred quid to wipe you off—I'm treating this as murder.'

I put the phone down very carefully into its soft, fur-lined nest.

CHAPTER TWO

Before I left, Vashni sang for me and, after Larri had murmured apologies and gone off about some business of his own, she danced. It was a strange dance performed in silence until the slow, stylized movement confused the senses and became sound. The basis was pure sexuality, but viewed from so broad a base that it was not a titilation but a statement of a wholeness that was utterly, irrevocably, female.

When she let me out into the warm London night, I was wading waist-deep in magic, my head swimming with a mixture of wine, ancient brandy, and desire. At the bottom of the steps I drew a deep shuddering breath; my lungs choked on the used, greasy air of the long, hot, day, and I walked swiftly down to the river, turning along the Embankment towards home. Cool draughts coiled up from the racing, black water.

Opposite the Millbank Tower I stopped and leaned on the parapet. At 2 a.m. the road behind, and the river in front were both deserted. The tide was newly turned, and, just out of reach of my hand, the twisting vortices of the ebb were ringed with rainbows of spilt oil, catching up light from a solitary window high in the glass and concrete monster behind me. A tug snuffled into view round the Westminster bend, dragging a string of barges —a water beast, its diesel heart thumping as it shoved its way against a million tons of polluted water sweeping silently to the sea.

A part of my drowsing mind picked up the familiar sound of a car drawing into the kerb. There must have been footsteps behind me, but if so, they failed to register. A moment later I was fighting for air, clawing frantically at a band of steel that had locked itself round my throat, wondering dully at a savage pressure on my spine. Pain gathered at the back of my head and exploded in white gouts of incandescent light through a vast web of neural paths. The senses melted and changed. I smelled the pressure on my throat, heard the acrid stink of human sweat, opened my eyes and saw, in streaks of red, the sound of men's muttering voices. I screamed, and the long, thin sound looped and wavered into blue patterns on a crimson sky.

The pressure had ceased. I opened my eyes and a golden hawk danced before them. Somewhere a whistle was blowing and the pavement echoed to pounding feet. I closed my eyes again and toppled thankfully back into the black softness of the river. As I fell, the car at the kerb gunned its motor and hurtled away, leaving behind a blue and dying pattern of screaming, tortured tyres.

My opportune policeman had his priorities right. He used his short wave radio instead of indulging in aquatic heroics and the river police picked me up before I had time to crack my head on the piers of Lambeth Bridge.

On the whole policemen do not like their quiet nights broken into by attempted murder, and if they can't catch the villains they may, understandably, show their irritation with the intended victim. As a member of the public I could, after being solicitously dried out and fussed over, have expected several hours of questioning. However, the uses of power are many and very sweet. As a member of the Government I was back in my own flat in ten minutes, dripping wetly towards the bathroom across my excellent Shiraz rugs.

The flat is unique; totally secluded and totally unexpected. It is approached through a maze of medieval cloisters and tunnels on the west flank of Westminster Abbey, and, when reached, a worn flight of grey stone steps climbs from a hidden garden to a five-hundred-year-old front door. I first heard of the place from a friend on the Abbey staff, and wanted it badly.

On the day I became Minister I determined to have it, and within a week I was able to do the authorities such a favour they would have been justified in letting me set up house in the Henry VII Chapel. I loved its remoteness. Not a sound penetrated here but the muffled crash of the hours from the great Westminster clock.

Usually I loathe crowds and noise, but tonight I could have done with a few more signs of humanity. Sharing a chalet in a packed holiday camp would have suited me perfectly. I was uneasily conscious of the fact that axemen could operate on my front door and no one but I would be any the wiser. I dropped the last of my sodden clothes in the bath and gingerly examined my throat in the mirrored wall.

A bright scarlet weal an inch wide circled my neck. The top of my spine creaked as I bent over the washbasin, my shoulders ached. I thought dully what a damnable way it was to kill a man. Why not simply crack me on the head and chuck the body in the water? And who were they? Politicians are not often loved; but two murder attempts in the same evening argued a quality of hate way out beyond the usual dull dislike of the citizen for his elected representatives. Both attempts had been really professional jobs.

I found my head dropping towards the running taps. Suddenly, enormously tired, I reeled into the bedroom. A faint scrabbling at the window slammed me awake in one heart-stopping second, and I dropped flat beside the bed with enough adrenalin in my blood to take on Mohammed Ali. The ancient leaded window creaked open and the tough, one-eared tom-cat I had taken over with the flat, slid swiftly into the room. I laughed unsteadily, and the laugh was too loud and went on for too long; then I put on a bathrobe and searched every corner in the place. I found myself bending to peer under the bed, and straightened up with a wry smile. Unless they were using two-dimensional dwarf assassins I was safe enough there.

I slopped Scotch into a glass, gagged it down and held out a hand to check my nerves. The dregs of the drink spilled out on the carpet.

I whispered *'Diawl!'* into the stillness and sat shakily on the bed, an image forming in the redness behind my eyes. A hawk, a blinding golden hawk. The telephone bludgeoned me back to consciousness. Lettcombe again, still respectful to the great man, but with more than an edge of impatience.

'Mr Traherne?'

'Yes.'

'The river police have reported to me and I've got the man off the beat here. I'm sending a car for you, sir—

or if you don't feel up to it we'll be round in ten minutes.'

'No.'

His voice was hard. 'Look, sir, with respect, I'm not going off my food if you *are* clobbered but I've got my duty to do and I intend doing it. My Assistant Commissioner's on my back already—and when they wake him up I'll have the Chief helping him. I'll be round in five minutes.'

As I put on dry clothes I tried to work out why I didn't want to talk to Lettcombe. Murder is a very personal activity—particularly when you are the intended corpse. A dull anger was lighting itself in my guts. Someone was trying to kill me, trying to turn my own much loved lump of living meat and reflexes into stinking corruption, and, whoever they were, I wanted them. I wanted them as I never wanted a woman but with the same flesh stirring passion. It was utterly illogical, but I would as soon have invited Lettcombe to watch me make love as to let him get between these Unknown and myself.

I picked up the still dripping coat, fished out my wallet, and spread it open on the dressing-table. A thin piece of paper was glued wetly across the back. I peeled it off, made to throw it away, and stopped. Something vaguely familiar had caught my eye. I pulled a few pieces of toilet paper from their nest and carefully blotted the sodden scrap. A blurred scrawl showed on the drying surface. The sense of familiarity puzzled me. I peered more closely, then carefully put the fragment down. It was unreadable, but no other language could crowd such improbable consonants together. I found I was thinking in Welsh and words stared up at me, *'Dieithriad—Craig y Meirw'*—an unreadable streak of ink then figures. A date? But anyway too far gone to recognize. I translated what I had ... 'Strangers'—foreigners perhaps?—'Dead Rock'. There was a good deal more, but whoever had written it was no calligraphy expert, and Thames water hadn't improved his work. I sat and thought hard. The last time I had used the wallet was at lunch in the House. There'd been a good many chances for someone to slip me that note since then. Was this something to do with the attacks on me? Had I perhaps stumbled on something so important to someone that I had to die before I took action on it? But what in hell *had* I found?

The door-bell shrilled and I started violently dropping the paper. As I stooped to pick it up, a word stood out like blue-rimmed fire from the blurred page, *'eryr'*—'eagle'. I went swiftly back into the bedroom, picked up my already packed suitcase, and slipped quietly out of the back-door. In falconry the eagle is the boss bird—but he's none the less a hawk.

My back-door leads out through a two-foot-wide passage in the thickness of the main Abbey wall and exits at a tiny postern opposite the vast ceremonial entrance to the House of Lords. I closed the postern door quietly behind me and stood very still. This was the dead hour. Three heavy lorries rumbled slowly round Parliament Square and passed me, heading for the long haul north. A thin ooze of traffic trickled from Whitehall and out over Westminster Bridge. A few hours later, the solid Norman curves of the Abbey and the Gothic fantasy of Parliament buildings would be dimmed in a haze of petrol fumes, and a man would cross the road at his peril.

I crossed safely enough now, and felt very small and far too conspicuous in that vast empty space. Someone wanted me dead. I'd faced trouble enough in my time. Everything from the early fist fights of Brynmawr to a hostile House backed by a snarling press. I always win, and you don't win in my game without guts, but I hadn't faced physical violence since my fighting youth. Now I was tired, so tired that my thoughts dragged themselves along the synapses of my brain like narcotized snails.

It would be a simple enough matter to get out and leave it all. Probably, whoever was after me, had got the wrong man—or it was some lunatic political fringe. All I had to do was pick up a cab to London Airport and sit in a brightly lit waiting area with a thousand other travellers until my plane was due, then I could lie in the sun while Lettcombe and his men sorted it out. A cab cruised past. I stopped it and sank back on the cushions; I was so sure of where I was going that I forgot to tell the driver. He shoved back the glass panel and asked, 'Where to then, Guv?'

I said wearily, '109 Eaton Square.'

Vashni opened the door. She didn't seem surprised to see me and, as I stood swaying in the hall, I offered no explanations. It was enough to be with her. She put an arm round me, said 'Bed' and led me up the great curve of the stairs. I tried to protest as she helped me shed clothes, but the only answer I got was, 'That's enough from you, my man—turn round.'

Later, she brought a strange spiced drink, and I slid away down an endless black tunnel. Infinities distant, in the bright mouth, sat a small golden bird.

I woke feeling wonderful. I have been a fighter all my life, and I carry the fight with me into sleep. Waking for me is always a matter of superimposing dream images and fears on to reality. Banishing them into the sub-conscious can lose valuable material—I've solved a lot of problems in the moment between sleep and waking. There were none to solve today. Consciousness surfaced diamond-clear in my mind, but I kept my eyes closed. Instead of petrol fumes I was breathing cool, sea-scented air, and the faintest breath of sandalwood that could only mean Vashni. I opened my eyes and looked up into her calm face. Under the pale skin of her throat a blue vein pulsed slowly.

I said, 'This where-am-I gag is wearing thin.'

'Don't worry: old gags are best; you've only been kidnapped.'

'Wales?'

She nodded. 'Wales.'

'I ought to be in Jamaica.'

She stared down at me. 'Would you like that?'

She was wearing an ankle-length green silk skirt, and a white high-necked blouse, just covering the nipple areas but open to the waist. I put up a hand and pushed the thin material aside. It seemed an entirely natural thing to do. She knelt swiftly beside the bed, pulled my head against her breasts, and held it fiercely. Through the open window I could hear the raucous cry of seagulls. After a few moments she kissed the top of my head, stood up, and tucked the blouse back into place. It was a casual, almost absent-minded action, performed by a woman so sure of her companion that she was careless whether she was watched or not.

'Come on,' she said, 'get up. Breakfast's ready and Dawa Chand hates to see his triumphs spoiled.'

I leapt out of the bed towards her, tripped and fell. The door slammed and I could hear her laughing as she ran down the corridor.

The man who redesigned the old stone house had reversed the natural order of Welsh architecture. The traditional coastal houses crouch under heavy slate roofs exposing minimum window space to the scouring sea winds. I reached the breakfast-room by following the laughter of Vashni and her brother, and when I pushed open the door I was part of the sea and sky. The room hung over a cliff, and two sides of it were one continuous sheet of glass. I looked cautiously down; three hundred feet below, miniature breakers clawed at toy red rocks.

Larri said, 'Good for the digestion; come and have some sea trout—Dawa caught it this morning.' Vashni filled my plate and all but sat on my lap as I ate. Occasionally she tried to feed me special pieces from her own plate.

'For goodness sake leave the man alone,' Larri said. 'Save your maternal instincts until they're needed—besides I want to talk to him before he calls the cops.'

She blushed furiously and moved to the very end of the table. I glanced over at her and the thought of leaving tied a knot in my guts. It was not sentimentality. My pulse rate was unaltered and, presumably, my blood pressure pursued its usual pattern. There was just a feeling of familiarity and deep need.

'What's worrying you?' I asked Larri.

'Are you all right now?'

'Yes, wonderful.'

'I don't want to pry,' he said hesitantly, 'but you're a toughish sort of man and yet you were out on your feet last night. It wasn't drink or that accident—something happened. I think perhaps that someone has taken a rather violent dislike to you.'

I made a swift decision, opened my wallet, and tossed the water blurred message to him. He studied it carefully and raised puzzled eyebrows.

'I'm sorry, my dear Holmes, the clue is rather incomplete.'

'How about the language, Dr Watson?'

'Ah, I see. Brilliant, my dear Holmes. Welsh of course. Note the diaeresis ...' He put the scrap down and anchored it under a coffee cup. 'What the hell does it mean, Traherne?' he asked seriously.

I ran through the scenario of my evening. When I finished he said quietly, 'I am glad and honoured that you came to us.'

I said bleakly, 'It's Welsh all right. What there is of it says "foreigners—dead rock". You make what you like of it—I have my own ideas.' For some reason I didn't mention the hawk.

Larri said cautiously, 'I, too, have an idea. It may sound a little coincidental but ... had you any trouble of this nature before you met us?'

'I've had trouble,' I said bluntly. 'You don't get to a position of damn nearly running a country by playing pat-a-cake with your enemies, but however much they may have wanted to, no one's tried to murder me before.

If you know anything it would be friendly to tell me. I've a lot of living to do yet.'

'I can't tell you much,' he said. 'I have only hints and suspicions to work on, but my people are afraid.'

Vashni had forgotten to be coy. 'You have Chota Dal to work on,' she said. 'He's a Sudra and totally unimportant—and I'm going to find him if I spend the rest of my life doing it.'

'Why?' I asked.

She was leaning forward, a strange intent expression on her face.

'It's not only Chota,' Larri said irritably. 'There are others.'

My eyes were fixed on her face. 'Why?' I asked again.

'Because he is nothing,' she said. 'Nothing and everything. A human life is worthless—and at the same time worth the universe.'

'Not a sparrow falls?' I tried to keep the cynicism out of my voice, but she picked it up.

'Sparrows as well if you like. The Part is the Whole, and the Whole the Part. They are identical and that is something the West does not yet know.'

For one timeless moment, as she stood her figure limned against the sea glare beyond the window, she seemed huge, filling the room with more than her human presence. Larri was staring back at her, black eyes glittering. She laughed suddenly and sat on the table swinging her legs. 'And I don't want you murdered, my man!' She ran a hand lightly through my hair. 'I've several uses for you.'

Larri looked interested but didn't comment.

I said, 'Look. Since I was elected I've had practically nothing to do with my Indian constituents. I know now I was wrong, so forget it; but as soon as I did, things started to happen. I meet you people; Vashni tells me about this missing young man, Chota; and I'm nearly murdered twice. I hadn't expected to come to Wales ever again, and here I am. And here you two are. Personally I think there are too many coincidences.'

A gull swooped at the food, saw his mistake an inch from the window, and tumbled down through the air, an indignant ball of feathers. Larri sighed and said, 'I wish you'd gone to Jamaica. More blacks for you I fear, but less trouble than us.'

'That's not fair,' I said furiously. 'You know perfectly well ...'

He glanced at Vashni. 'Yes,' he said, 'I know perfectly well. All right. Why do you think I have this house?' He waved a thin brown hand round the room. 'Since I started this work with my people I have learned many strange things, and I don't tell them all to the authorities.'

'Yes, Lettcombe loves you for that,' I said dryly.

He waved an impatient hand. 'I knew, long ago, the immigrants were being exploited, but, until recently, I didn't know how much. Now I do know I have to do something about it.'

'*You* might,' I said sourly. 'But why am I involved?'

'Why indeed should you care what happens to a parcel of bloody wogs?'

We sat glaring at each other but it was I who looked away. 'I do now,' I said uneasily.

He rose swiftly and put an arm round my shoulders.

'I'm sorry,' he said. 'We are an excitable race. Look, you took an interest in Chota Dal. Well, he's nothing—he probably thinks of himself as dirt—but we happen to think he could be a very important pawn in the game. His mother wrote to Vashni, but I heard from another source. I think he was coming over to see me.'

The plot was thickening like mulligatawny soup. I remembered, uneasily, the fight on the embankment—and thought about trains to London. Vashni brought me abruptly back to the present.

'I don't want to find him just for that,' she said passionately. 'He is a man; isn't that reason enough to help him?'

I looked at her and found she was reason enough for me to forget London, my ambition, and my life. Larri was speaking, and I came back to him with some difficulty.

' ... so something appalling is going on, and the key to it is here.'

'Are you sure?'

'Yes, and you've earned the right to be told the truth. In any case you're not naïve enough to believe that Dawa found this house by accident. I'm dead certain the illegals in London came through this area, and that's why we are here.'

'I hope you know what you're doing,' I said heavily. 'I presume we are not dealing with fools; they must know you are here.'

'They do.'

I made my decision in that moment. From my normal standpoint it was madness, but I knew I had no choice.

'I'm not given to false modesty,' I said; 'I'm tough, I have power, and I'll help.'

'Thank you. But why should you? You've had two very clear warnings; why don't you take your holiday and forget us?'

I said flatly, 'You know why.'

He looked at Vashni and sighed. 'Yes,' he said, 'you cannot step outside your Karma.'

He grinned suddenly and held his hand out across the table. 'I shall be most grateful for your assistance, Holmes my dear fellow.'

'Anyway,' Vashni said briskly, 'I'll soon know what Chota looks like.'

'You will? Good Lord, how?' Larri barked.

She smiled sweetly at him. 'I'm brilliant. Go on, admit I'm brilliant and I'll tell you.'

'You're a Jat buffalo,' Larri said, and added something in Urdu.

She laughed aloud and held out both hands to him. For one long moment they stood, hands linked, dark heads thrown back, inevitable partners frozen in the dance, twin poles of a dynamo, opposite and the same, the air between them sparked with power. The pose broke, and they whirled, smiling, towards me. I took her hands. It seems fanciful but I swear a charge passed from her into my body.

'You're beautiful *and* brilliant,' I said shakily. 'Now tell us about Chota.'

She left her hands in mine; one index finger traced a brief intricate pattern on my palm. The pale olive face was very near; she looked thoughtfully at me. 'You're

39

not used to flattering women, are you? Very well, I rang Eaton Square this morning and there is a letter for me. Chota's mother has found two photographs: one of him and one of his father.'

'Well if you pull your haystack to pieces now,' Larri said, 'you'll at least recognize the needle.'

'Why wouldn't *you*?' I asked. 'You must have known him in India.' I still held Vashni's hands. At that moment it would have seemed something against nature to have let her go.

Larri shrugged. 'He went south when he was quite young, right down into Madras, I believe. There were some relations down there—I seem to remember giving permission for him to go.' He looked embarrassed. 'But, you know, things are different in India—a sweeper's boy ... oh, I try, but caste ...' he hesitated. 'Look, you can't eradicate three thousand years of tradition by passing laws. It's in our blood. He is a Sudra; I was not only his hereditary Rajah, but my caste is Kshatriya. If he were brought to my notice I'd see him. Otherwise ...' he sighed. 'I think I do remember him as a little boy—he was bullied a bit. Yes, I remember finding him weeping one day. He'd hidden in the old throne-room. No right to be there at all of course ...'

'And you completely lost track of him since then?' I asked incredulously.

'I know it's difficult to believe,' he said uncomfortably. 'I probably saw him hundreds of times after that but one just wouldn't notice; he would be so unimportant ...'

Vashni and I spent the day together exploring Pen-

Clawdd Isle, which is not a true island but a small peninsula owned entirely by Larri and projecting a mile out to sea. Except where the narrow neck joins the mainland it is bounded by towering, sea-washed cliffs. The house is perched on the northern heights, and can be reached only from the village via a narrow road of pulverized rock.

Looking west was like staring into an analogue of Infinity. Sea and sky mixed together, pouring silently over the curvature of the planet. To the east the land fell abruptly to the neck, then rose gently to the foothills of the Prescellys. Two long fingers of narrow, wooded valley poked up into the green hide of the higher slopes. The road on the far side of the village showed a brief hump-backed curve before plunging into one of these to reappear in the far distance, a tiny wrinkle in the smooth mountain face.

We tramped through heather and broken rock, scrambled down vertiginous cliff paths, and sunned ourselves on dizzy ledges.

About midday we found ourselves on a ledge ten feet above the waves. The sea had carved a pool from the rock, deep, misty with weed and filled by every tide.

Vashni said, 'Why haven't I found this before? What a place to swim!' She looked at me, speculation in her eyes. 'I don't altogether trust you,' she said. 'I'm going first. There's a lovely view out to sea—mind you keep admiring it.'

I heard the rustle of clothing behind me then silence. I might have adopted the shibboleths of England but Welsh blood was stronger. I turned my head.

Outlined against the rock she was part of it. An archaic bas-relief: face lifted to the sky rapt and secret; hands linked behind her head, holding the hair, a bar of ebony falling from the crown, clear of the arched back, to the rock at her feet; the great, gravity-defying curve of breasts, arrogantly tipped, standing out from the deep rib cage; the impossibly slender waist flaring to rounded hips and strong dancer's thighs; legs tapering to tiny narrow feet.

Whenever she moved she made all other women I have ever seen look like milking cows, but now, in her immobility, there was frozen movement, a restrained power, frightening in its intensity. She was no longer Vashni but all femaleness from the dim beginning of life. I put my fingers to my mouth. She caught the movement from the corner of her eye. Her hands flashed down to cover the black silk of pubic thatch, then she laughed and vanished into the pool. A twisting plunge, graceful as a diving seal.

After the swim we sat munching hunks of flat, unleavened Welsh bread and a pungent local cheese. We drank from a stream feathering down to the sea from two hundred feet above and talked incessantly, raking out small forgotten details of our lives. For me it was like deep analysis and had the same calming effect. There were a good many things I would have sooner left under their stones, but she accepted everything without comment and, as they scuttled out into the sunlight, they seemed somehow less ugly.

Her life had been quiet enough. With her parents dead she had been reared by whispering court women in the vast, crumbling, sun-baked palace of her people. By the time Larri sent her to England she had learned many curious by-ways of human behaviour. She exchanged it all for the hygenic austerity of an English boarding-school returning only for the holidays.

Outside the palace the new political torrents had washed Larri contemptuously out of their path. He had now no official power but, when necessary, he defended his lost subjects against the bureaucrats of central government who regarded him with considerable suspicion. Nothing was too much trouble for him to take for the most poverty-stricken and abject bundle of humanity. The search for Chota Dal was a typical case. When Vashni left school he spent more and more time in England helping im-migrants and getting a bad name with the Home Office for withholding information.

I knew he was indecently rich. Vashni had no idea where it all came from but, like leprechauns, every Rajah of the old régime gathered his crock of gold, and she assumed Larri had converted some ancient jewelled hoard from the palace strong-rooms into more modern currency, before the republic could get its hands on it.

Towards evening we were lying on a ledge under the lip of the western cliffs. A wind sang overhead, but here it was like being inside a vast heated room. The slopes of purple rock and broken scree had stored the warmth of the day and now flung it back towards the dull red furnace of the setting sun.

I stood up, yawned, and said, 'We'd better get back. Larri will wonder what I'm doing with you.'

However much we had talked there had been a curious physical shyness between us all day. I put out my hand to haul her to her feet, but she avoided it and scrambled up by herself. A heavy, booming thud shuddered up through the rock.

She said, 'Tide's coming in; it's the sea in the caves; the shoreline is like a honeycomb.'

The words were ordinary enough but her voice was high-pitched and strange. For a moment she stood with her hands clenched into tight fists then she spoke again, a nasal, formal chant in words I could not understand. I moved towards her but she joined her hands and fell at my feet, head bowed, the long, black strands of hair shadow bars against the rock. As I tried to lift her she made a curious gesture, touching my right foot and my knees with her right hand, the left hand holding the right elbow; then she rose swiftly, palms together against her breast.

She said thickly, 'You are my lord, take or leave.'

Her upturned face was rapt, the heavy eyelids closed. It was a formula older than my own ancient race. On that bright Welsh hilltop it should have been absurd, but I took her head in my hands, kissed her closed eyes then, very gently, her mouth. She tasted strange, sweet yet bitter and very foreign.

I asked, 'Should I say something?'

She shook her head. 'No. That is acceptance. How did you know?'

I said, 'I don't know anything today.'

Out in the bay a speedboat executed figures of eight and the muted roar of its engine echoed up the cliff.

She laughed suddenly. 'I know one thing. If I don't go and chase Dawa we'll be eating curried sheep again.'

I started to scramble up from the ledge.

'No, stay here,' she said, and ran towards the house.

CHAPTER THREE

I stayed on the ledge until dark. I had a lot to think about.
I had met this woman three days ago, I had barely
touched her and, at this point in my career, I needed to be
tied up with an Indian girl about as much as I needed
several vertical holes drilled in the top of my head; and
she was part of me. As much part of me as my arms or
my legs or my bowels.

An hour later I climbed up into the cool night wind
and tripped over something that cried out like a trapped
hare and struck upwards into my crotch. Through the
pain mist I remembered to tuck my shoulder down and
roll—I'd saved my collar bone a good many times with
that one on the rugby field. I ended fifteen feet away flat
behind a rock, while the thing on the ground muttered
and clawed through the heather towards me. I backed
away shivering, then the last of the evening light picked
out a contorted brown face. I stayed behind my rock until
he came level then heaved my whole weight sideways on
to his back. The air whistled out of him like a burst tyre.
I slid a hand down his arm, gripped the thin wrist, and
jerked a long knife out of his fist. He had hit me with the
handle and I was grateful for his consideration. Private
parts are so called for a very good reason and I didn't
fancy mine being exposed to six inches of steel. I turned
my catch over and examined it. At his peak he wouldn't
have got far in a beefcake competition. The way he was

now, Evans the Death back in Brynmawr would have had his tape measure out. His knees and bare feet were clotted with blood; a thin cotton shirt, ripped to shreds, revealed bones pushing their way through mottled brown skin; a few rags that had been trousers hung from his waist by a ravelled length of string. He had left a trail over the heather like a wounded animal. I back-tracked to the cliff top; there was no doubt about it, he had come up that near vertical face from the sea. I tried to pick him up and the pain in my crotch bent me double. I put my face down near his and said clearly, 'I am going for help—wait here—you are safe now, do you understand?'

He looked blankly at me and I stumbled back towards the house.

I couldn't find Vashni or her brother and I didn't waste time looking for them. Dawa Chand was pottering in the dining-room moving silver about and standing back twitching his rabbit nose at the effect. I shouted at him to grab something for a stretcher and ran back to the phone in the hall. I lost a few minutes finding the number of the local policeman; it was hidden in a pencilled, ancient maze of information on a wall pad and eventually I tracked it down overwritten by a cryptic message that said 'sausages'.

I imagine I had brought the law away from his evening meal and he wasn't very pleased, but he got the message eventually and I trotted off through the heather with Dawa following reluctantly, an old door balanced on his turban. He was a nice little man, but nervous; when he heard the boom of the sea in the caves he dropped his burden and tried to run.

My rock was still there but my man had gone. He seemed to have been a tidy-minded character for Dawa's torch showed no sign of his track. Either the heather had been carefully brushed upright or I'd got the wrong rock. I was still thinking that one out when the policeman arrived with Larri and we used his torch to peer down into the black gulf over the cliff edge. It was a good torch but showed no crushed body on the sea-licked rocks below.

An hour later we had covered all the obvious places on the peninsula. Unless he was hiding in a hole my tourist had gone down to the village or taken to the mountains. Back at the house I insisted that an official statement be taken but the policeman's heart wasn't in it and he left cursing under his breath in Welsh; it's a difficult language to swear in but he made a good workmanlike job of it.

Vashni was in her room and I didn't disturb her. An idea was growing in my mind and I wanted very badly to look at the coast below that cliff. For that I would need a boat. I'd been made to look quite enough of a fool already that evening so I kept my brilliant deductions to myself, slipped out of the house and walked down towards the lights of the village. There was little enough of it but what there was was good. It was plain as a Welshcake; unspoiled by planners and the creeping tide of caravans that has maggoted over the lovely sands farther south. A thin straggle of slate-roofed houses wandered down a hillside and spilled over on to a badger-grey pier, their whitewashed faces turned to the water, backs pressed into the hill behind.

South, across from the pier, the steep sides of Pen-Clawdd towered shutting out the Atlantic weather. The road to the house was just visible on its flank, a grey thread vanishing behind outcrops of rock and reappearing yards farther up. The whole place was sheltered from all winds but the north, and the one wide, cobbled street lay quiet as a sleeping dog in the warm evening air. I passed a tall Bethesda chapel—iron railings and God-fearing plainness—a litter of grey-hatted tombs in a shroud of grey grass. A false tooth in the natural smile of the street.

I met no one, but net curtains twitched aside as I passed. The pub was at the far end of the pier. Only true Welsh bloody-mindedness could have thought of that. Three fathoms of cold sea water six feet from its door—to sober the Saturday night sinners. There was no inn sign. A battered board nailed over the door announced that Ogden Rhys was licensed to sell something that the sea had long ago wiped clear. Smoke and the rumble of voices drifted through the open window. I ducked under the lintel. There were about twenty men packed in the small room, and one woman behind the bar. I entered and the hubbub of voices stopped dead. A good deal of it had been English but when I clattered over the polished floor it started up again in pure Welsh.

I called cheerfully, 'A large Scotch please, miss.'

She was a beautiful girl: huge grey eyes set wide above the high aristocratic cheekbones of a clear, pale face. I had forgotten the loveliness of Welsh women.

No one looked at me. A small, blue-jerseyed fisherman dumped his glass on the bar and I asked quickly, 'Will you have a drink?' He peered at me, from under shaggy eyebrows; a cunning, ancient face, kippered by the sea.

A man nearby said swiftly in Welsh, 'Drink with him, man.'

Kipper face turned back to me. 'Aye,' he said. 'Generous that is,' then to the girl, 'A pint, Mari,' but she had already filled the glass. He drank and asked politely, 'On holiday, is it?'

'Yes.'

He thought that one over; then, 'Down at Newport you'd be?'

'No,' I said, 'Pen-Clawdd.'

I made too good a job of the pronunciation and he looked sharply at me. 'Up by there?' He called out in English to no one in particular, 'Gentleman is staying up at the House.'

The crowd round the bar thinned as the men drifted over to watch two youths playing darts, and, from ten feet away, I stared into the face of the ugliest man I have ever seen. I weigh over 190 pounds stripped, this man was half as big again, and none of it was fat. Broad as a bull across the shoulders his white seaman's jersey showed muscle, bunched and swelling along arms as thick as a normal man's thigh. A great shaven spherical head was set virtually neckless into the shoulder muscles. He swung round towards me. I suppose he was used to frightening strangers with that face, but I am not a poker player and a politician for nothing. I nodded politely and said, 'Good evening.'

I have never expected much from people in the way of looks. With the myriad chances of ancestry and birth it seems enough to me that a man should emerge from the genetic whirlpool looking human. This man did not. As

I stared I saw that I had been mistaken and the head was not shaved: there was simply no trace of hair—no eyebrows—no lashes. The curve of the sphere was barely flattened to accommodate rudimentary features. There were no external ears, just two pink naked holes, and small circular colourless eyes were set so far apart as to appear almost touching them. The unnatural expanse of pink flesh between the eyes and the tiny amorphous blob that served as a nose was indescribably horrifying; but it was the mouth, in combination with the whole, that set the nerves screaming and dug ancient antipathies from the primaeval sludge of the brain. Beautiful lips, softly curved, red and sensual as an erotic dream parted showing strong even teeth.

'Good evening to you,' he said, and the voice was low and pleasantly modulated; an accent, not Welsh, thickened the consonants of the words.

I swallowed my drink and walked towards him. He stood as I approached, towering above me, the great Halloween mask of the head tilted forward away from the low ceiling. The nightmare mouth opened as he smiled sweetly and held out his hand. I was ready, and it was as well that I was. I had played this game with my father since I was six—and he had hands that could crush green apples to pulp. There is, of course, a trick in the hand-gripping game and without it I should have been on my knees in seconds. The idea is to hold your opponent's hand in such a way that the force he exerts is transferred back through the fulcrum of his own knuckles.

As our palms met I saw the idle knots of muscle on his

arm leap and writhe, and with nine-tenths of that dreadful force turned back to him my hand stiffened and cracked, and fire snaking from my wrist burst into the agonized shoulder muscles. The murmur of Welsh had ceased: there was not a sound in the room. The girl behind the bar had both hands pressed to her mouth.

I dragged my mind from the pain in my shoulder, smiled pleasantly, and said, 'Are you on holiday, too, or do you live here?'

For a second, surprise creased the smooth pink skin of the head. I knew he was not yet really trying and waited for the surge of power that could crush my hand to a bag of skin and broken chips of bone. Then the pressure was gone and he turned to the terrified bar girl.

'Whisky for my friend, and for me,' he said and stood erect, the ball of his head pressing the ceiling. *'Prosit!'* The neat Scotch was thrown between the smiling lips and the glass slammed on the counter.

I said, 'Cheers!' in my best middle-class English and drank. There was a communal sigh; someone said, *'Duw!'* quietly, and the bar returned to normal. I picked up his glass, said, 'Permit me,' and slid it towards the girl. She filled it and placed it cautiously in front of him. This time he sipped it delicately.

'Thank you,' he said. 'No, I am not Welsh, my friend, just an old German sailor. I have frequent business in Cardiff and come up here for the quiet—and to see my friends.'

He stared arrogantly round the bar. Everyone was earnestly talking to his neighbour; the clichés that come so easily in Welsh flew about the room.

A feather of excitement brushed my mind. Behind the seeming normality there was something wrong; something indefinable. A web of interest beyond the common round held these people together.

'Very good friends.' The wonderful smile came again. 'Kommer,' he said. 'My name is Kommer.' He held out his hand again and I took it without hesitation, trying no tricks. The handshake was gentle and warm.

I said, 'I am very pleased to meet you, Captain. My name is Traherne.'

'You know my rank?' he sounded pleased and surprised.

'I would not expect such a man to be a deckhand.'

He roared with laughter and crashed a vast hand between my shoulders. 'Deckhand! That is good. Do you know the sea?'

I said I had sailed a good deal, which was true enough. After a while I found the impact of those horrific features wore off. He had an extraordinary animal magnetism and I found I was enjoying his company.

The pale eyes peered shrewdly at me. 'Where do you work when you are not on leave?' he asked suddenly.

'London.'

He took a piece of paper from a hip pocket, snapped his fingers and said, 'Pencil.' The barmaid hurriedly took one from the old-fashioned cash register and put it in his fingers. He scrawled on the paper and pushed it towards me.

'If you find your work tedious when you return to London, go there. You will make some money.'

'I make quite a lot now, Captain,' I said mildly.

'Not this sort of money,' he said. 'Hard work, but *real* money. You will be surprised.'

'Why me?' I asked.

He turned and called sharply, 'Owen! Gwallter!'

Two of the fishermen shuffled out of the crowd. They were big men. He put a hand in each one's leather belt, effortlessly lifted them off the floor, then dropped them back on their heels.

'I am strong?' he asked.

I said, 'Excuse me,' reached across him and gripped the men by a loose fold of their clothes. A moment later I had them off the floor and lying along the flat of my forearms. I put them gently down and Kommer smashed a hand again between my shoulders.

'That is why,' he said. 'I am surrounded by weaklings.'

'What's the work?' I asked.

'Import—export,' he said, and pushed through the men to the door.

With the giant gone the strain went out of the atmosphere. The men drifted away from their tight, muttering knots and spread themselves on benches. The darts game became noisier. I called the girl over, bought another drink and said casually, 'What an extraordinary man—who is he?'

She slapped my change on the counter, snapped, 'He is Captain Kommer, sir,' and moved to the end of the bar, polishing glasses furiously.

I had come down to the pub to hire a boat. I wanted to look from the sea at the far side of the headland where my Indian had vanished. Ynysdeullyn lived by fishing; there were two score assorted craft packed in the little harbour and most of the owners were in the bar. I tried for an hour then gave up. The excuses were interesting; several of the men even professed not to understand English, but the fact remained that, in a poor community not one of those boat-owners would take good money for a few hours hire. I walked thoughtfully back up the dusk draped street, the curtains twitching again as I passed the little lighted windows.

Up at the house Larri sent apologies to the dinner table. He was working on a report for his welfare committee. I was pleased to have Vashni to myself, and while we ate, gave her a lively account of trying to hire a boat at the pub. For some reason I left out the German giant. She listened politely but hardly spoke a word. When we left the table I tried to take her hand and she pulled roughly away. I hadn't realized until then how much I had let down my defences. The food I had eaten curdled inside me as my stomach contracted. I said harshly, 'Now look here ...'

'I am afraid we must go back to London,' she interrupted. 'Larri has some unexpected business. Would you mind getting up early?' She crossed to the door and turned. She liked to wear a sari in the evenings and under it her body moved like molten silver. The knot in my guts tightened.

'You will want to get away on your holiday,' she said. 'Good night.'

I spent two hours in bed then got up and put my head under a cold tap. Normally I sleep like a back-bencher at a Treasury debate, but the knot of fear would not unroll. I felt abandoned and lost. For thirty-five years I had thought of little but Tomas Traherne and the splendid uniqueness of him. A man born to rule—and by God he was going to do it. A man not to be moved by petty emotions and the troubles of unimportant, crowded units of humanity; now a small incivility from a young girl was making me physically sick; I walked out on to the terrace that circled the house, a wind was nosing up from the north. Far below, long silver-capped rollers swept gracefully into the mouth of the harbour—moving like her body—the whisper of their breaking drifting up to my ears.

I shook my head and forced thought into an orderly pattern. When I left this damned place tomorrow I'd never return. Wales had always contrived to get under my skin. I would go straight to the airport and wait for the next vacant seat on a Jamaica-bound plane; take my well-earned holiday, then get back to my job. I'd drawn a great many threads together in the last few wakeful hours, but it was a knot Lettcombe could untie—he was paid for it and I'd had enough. I knew now why I had been attacked and I had a shrewd idea of what I'd stumbled on, but covering tracks by killing a cabinet minister suggested something very much bigger than I had thought possible.

Now Larri and Vashni ... my thought stopped there. I looked east; the Prescelly peaks were islanded in a flood of moonlight. Bright threads of water wavered down their flanks to the lush valley darkness below. What a land it was, clinging like a woman, leading the mind to soft warm places ... I stumbled back to my room and fell on the bed. Lights flashed over the ceiling. The engine of a car revved under the open French window and muttered away down the steep track. I wondered vaguely who was going out at that time of night, but I was too weary to be really interested.

Dawa Chand woke me, his gentle, rabbit face twitching anxiously above a breakfast tray. He put a table on the terrace and stayed to serve me. The usual mahogany brown of his broken face was grey, the eyes red-rimmed. He handed me coffee, stumbled, and the cup fell from his hand. In an instant he was on his knees.

'That I should fail the twice born ...'

I said sharply, 'Get up Dawa. When did you last sleep?'

'I sleep well, Sahib, always well.'

'You look like the wrath of God,' I said. 'Clear this up and go and get some rest.'

He was an engaging little man working himself to death for others and I was sorry for him.

I've encountered more hilarious situations than the drive back to London. Dawa Chand dozed beside the chauffeur, and, back in our glass box with Vashni between us, Larri and I chatted pleasantly of this and that. He was a formidable talker and a wonderful host but all we needed was a coffin to slip Vashni in and a couple of tall black hats and it would have made a very passable funeral cortège. She sat bolt upright staring over Dawa's sagging shoulders. Even when we stopped for a sumptuous picnic in a high, hanging wood in the Cotswolds she didn't utter a word. Eventually Larri shrugged, lifted his hands helplessly behind her back and lapsed into silence.

They dropped me at the main Abbey gate and I went in past the yard beadle who seemed surprised to see me.

I remembered I had given him a key and told him to look after the cat for a month, but he was a very tactful man and said nothing. I didn't need intuition to tell me I was being tailed; the slightest noise is multiplied in the cloisters. The phone was ringing as I opened the door. I picked it up and said, 'All right, Lettcombe, I can give you an hour—then I'm catching a plane. I'll come to you.'

As I put the instrument down it rang again. I swore softly; if my office had found me I'd be all day shaking them off. Vashni's voice came hurried and frightened from the receiver.

'Can I see you before you leave?'

'Why?'

'I'll come to the airport.'

'Why the renewed interest? I thought I'd become untouchable.' There was a long pause and I thought she had hung up. I called, 'Vashni, Vashni are you there ...?' When at last she answered her voice was almost too low for me to catch the words:

'No. I do not need to see you. Please go straight to your plane. It will be much better if you do that—promise me you will do that, Tomas.'

She had not called me that before.

'Come on now, Vashni, what's happened?'

'You remember the letter waiting for me with photographs of Chota and his father?'

'Yes.'

'Nothing else in the house is disturbed, but the letter has gone. Tomas, I'm frightened.'

I put the receiver down on the table. I knew that if I picked it up again I would probably have thrown away what had taken fifteen years of ruthless intrigue, fighting, and work to build. Up to this moment I could walk out. In a month's time I could put my bottom back on the front bench with no more complications than wondering if the next political axe-man was sitting beside me or over with the Opposition. In either case I was ready for them; when the House rose at the end of the session I knew that I could walk back in for the next as prospective leader—with an Indian national as a wife?

The receiver made impatient noises; I picked it up and said, 'Come to my flat in an hour's time.'

She said, 'Yes, Tomas' and the line went dead.

It takes five minutes to walk from my door to the shiny new headquarters of the Metropolitan Police. When I stood at the reception desk I couldn't remember how I had got there, and crossing Victoria Street in that frame of mind doesn't put you high up on an actuarial list. Lettcombe was busy and he wasn't wasting time on a mere cabinet minister.

'My Chief has put me in charge of you, Mr Traherne. You're my personal responsibility.'

He didn't bother to convince me of how delighted he was at the prospect. A girl came in with two cups of something that seemed to have been brewed from acorns; she slapped them down on the desk and went out. Lettcombe swallowed his in two gulps looking as though he wished it were hemlock, then pushed a piece of paper towards me.

'Times of flights to Jamaica,' he said. 'I've assigned a man to you—he'll see you safe until you're aboard.'

'Suppose I'm too busy to go?'

He looked coldly across the desk. 'You are going,' he said. 'Don't argue with me. When you're Prime Minister I'll probably lose my pension. If you pick up that phone to my Chief he'll give me orders to obey you, then break me when you're clobbered by this lot. I lose both ways so you're catching a plane today.'

'Of course, Chief Inspector—but tomorrow.'

He blinked. 'Do you really mean that?'

'Of course—and when I'm P.M. you'll lose your present pension all right. I believe Assistant Commissioners are on a different scheme.'

He was a good man, cold-headed, but a great deal more honest than me, and I hated what I was doing to him. He sat back beaming delightedly.

'Have some more coffee.'

I told him I thought it would be dangerous to exceed the prescribed dose and got up to go.

'Please sit down, sir,' he said happily. 'I expect you'd like to know how far we've got with this?'

I did want to know very badly. With what I had to do I didn't just need to know who the opposition were. If I were going to stay alive I needed the lot, including when they wound up their watches and the brand name on their toilet paper.

'That's very kind of you,' I said.

Lettcombe ticked the facts off on his fingers. 'We picked up the driver of that truck. Not much there. He was to get five hundred quid for writing you off. He met his contact in a dark room and was given a hundred pounds on account. He's got form—robbery with violence. He'll get life if I can pin murder on him, but his counsel will probably get it altered to manslaughter and he'll get five years—and that's the end of the line there. Number two attempt. No clue whatever except the man on the beat swears they were all coloured men who attacked you. Now I'm linking this back with your past history. You have no trouble until you take an interest in your coloured constituents. Then you start talking about illegal immigration; you link up with Prince Larishnapur, and certain people start getting very unfriendly towards you. They reason that you're powerful enough to get a major campaign going which will smash their racket—so you'd better be dead.'

I interrupted him. 'But surely Larishnapur is ...'

'Larishnapur knows what's going on. He knows a damned sight more than us and he won't tell. He won't tell because he's basically one of the best men I've ever met. These poor bastards of immigrants are in trouble. If we catch 'em they're deported—and if we don't they still haven't got it made; either way they're up to their necks with the money-lenders and it's very unhealthy to miss a payment.'

'Larri could help you a lot,' I said. 'Perhaps you haven't tackled him the right way.'

He slammed his hand down and the coffee cup spilled its dubious dregs on his blotter. 'Larishnapur wants it *both* ways,' he roared. 'He's trying to crack the racket on his own *and* protect the illegal immigrants. He'll do anything to help them including breaking the law, and he'll end up dead and get me into more trouble. If I had my way I'd deport him and his sister, but with the contacts he's got I might as well try and deport the House of

60

Lords.' He broke off. 'Why you haven't finished your coffee, sir.'

I told him I thought it was a bit rich for that time of day and he pulled the cup towards him and sipped thoughtfully as he spoke. 'The old racket was broken three years ago and I still swear nothing could get through on the south coast, but this is new. We're dealing with a very large scale, highly organized operation. A new batch came in this week; we picked up five in your own manor and they were a fraction of what really came. I chanced my arm and promised 'em they could stay if they talked, but they hadn't a damned clue where they'd been or what they came in—they even thought they'd been swindled and dumped back on the Continent.'

'Why?'

'The people who brought 'em up from the coast were white but they weren't speaking English—could be the whole thing is Continental based.'

I got up to go and he shook hands warmly. 'I'm sorry we had our differences, sir.'

'I meant that about Assistant Commissioner, Mr Lettcombe,' I said. 'By the way, what action *are* you taking on Larishnapur?'

'I've already warned him, and if only for his sister's sake, I'll do it again—but he won't cause me much more trouble.'

I had my hand on the door handle and I turned back towards him. 'Why?' I asked.

'Because they'll both be dead,' he said flatly. 'They're amateurs and they don't stand a chance.'

*   *   *

When I got back to the flat the beadle had let Vashni in. I walked into the sitting-room and she rose from the sofa, wrapped her arms round me, and buried her face in my neck. I held her and her body melted into mine, limbs and trunk, soft and part of me. Home and safety. I said lightly, 'Careful, love, you're strong as a bear,' but my voice was shaking.

She moaned and turned up her face; then her mouth caught mine and I drowned away from the world. Thirty-five years of existence and I had never before been aware of the actual living reality of another human being. I had lived without empathy: nothing real but myself; everything round me a personal dream to be manipulated as I chose; people were objects to be used. Now this.

Then, somehow she was under me, her softness the softness of all women since the beginningless beginning of the Race. She lifted her head from the floor, eyes wide, mouth twisted as though with pain and said, 'Take me! Oh, my Lord, take me!'

There was a cry. A high, triumphant, singing sound, and another blended with it. A crystal helix of sound climbing from duality to oneness.

It is hard to be born.

I lifted my head and looked slowly round that familiar room. The twist and fall of the curtains held the secret heart of the Universe; the spines of my books flashed and glittered in colours new-made in that timeless instant. I looked down and the world was a perfection of one bright, erect, rose nipple mounted on an aureole of purple.

I whispered, 'Oh, Vashni; Vashni *cariad*!'

'It's a beautiful language,' she said drowsily. 'You must

teach me.' Then, 'Darling, you're lying exactly where you belong and don't ever forget it—but I feel like a pancake.'

We dressed holding hands—there are easier ways—and we ended in a helpless, laughing heap on the sofa. She lay in my lap, her head under my chin.

I said, 'Stop purring; that much complacency is indecent.'

She cupped my face in her hands. 'Got you!' she said. 'And I'll purr all I like; I'm home.'

'We both are,' I said. 'But what now?'

There was not a vestige of doubt left in my mind, but the rejection of last night still puzzled me. She answered my thought with uncanny precision.

'Darling, I had to pretend so that you would go away and be safe. You are in dreadful danger if you stay here.'

'How the hell did you know what I was thinking?' This time she had really startled me.

The full lips curled in a secretive smile. 'You'll get used to it, my love; we have never existed as two people.'

'I can think of times when that could be downright embarrassing,' I said; but I thought about it and she was right. It was going to alter my basic way of life; smash my carefully worked out plan for survival on my own terms; then I remembered Lettcombe's parting words.

'Now look,' I said harshly, 'this lot aren't playing kiss-in-the-ring. If you go on working with Larri you're in bad trouble. You're going to get out of this and stay out.'

'If I go away,' she said thoughtfully, 'fly to India for a few weeks, will you go to Jamaica as you'd planned until the police have settled this?'

'Yes,' I said quickly, 'I'll go along with that, and we mustn't get in touch until we're both back here. Whoever they are they're pros and they're tough. I don't want them tracing you. What about Larri?'

Her face clouded. 'I can't stop Larri,' she said sadly. 'No one can.'

There was plenty of food in the freezer. We had a lot of discovering to do; most of the time it seemed like rediscovery of old and forgotten joy. We stayed where we were until morning.

Vashni was to catch an afternoon plane, and at ten o'clock I put her in a taxi for Eaton Square. I had not realized what it was going to be like. As she drove away I felt exactly as though someone had drained my entire gallon ration of blood. Someone caught my arm and, out of a red mist a voice asked, 'Are you all right, sir?' I shook my head and shambled across the road to the ornate Victorian pub that lurks under the skirts of New Scotland Yard.

Two drinks later I still hadn't caught up on what had happened to me. I thought dully that if this was the result of my revelation I could have struggled along without it; then suddenly she was back. Like the returning flow in a blocked artery she surged, a river of joy, through the stagnant blood. The illusion was so powerful that I blinked my eyes expecting to see her beside me.

The bar was alive with beauty: bottles flamed like jewels, warm emotion glowed in the faces round me. The strangeness of the obvious overwhelmed me. I looked through the open door and saw with new found wonder that the wheels of the passing cars were round. I must have spoken aloud for the barman said pityingly, 'That's right, mate, if they was square you'd never get the bleedin' tyres on.'

CHAPTER FOUR

Lettcombe's man fell into step beside me as I left the pub. He was a pleasant young man with enough facial hair to have driven an old-time senior officer up the nearest wall. He wore sandals in place of regulation boots and, on the principle of hiding in the limelight, his clothes were Carnaby Street cowboy. In London he didn't warrant a second glance. He was the new C.I.D.; with it, intelligent, and tough. I thought, nostalgically, of the old bovine blue-suited model. With this one I was going to have to think fast.

My luggage had gone off that morning and would be aboard the aircraft before we reached Heathrow. We took the new tube line and were in Reception in twenty minutes. The sweet smell of power wafted us through to V.I.P. quarters where I had to pose for a few photographers and produce platitudes for bored reporters; then we sat down and I had a drink on the Management. Fur Face was on duty and refused, but he did it artistically.

At ten minutes to take-off time I got restless. There were six other people in the lounge and I didn't know one of them; just then I needed an acquaintance badly. I got one at E.T.D. minus five by which time I was really worried. Willie Wyndham. Society columnist, writer for women's magazines, gardening expert. His line was 'I love Mum'; he sprinkled it with roses and ten million women cooed over the syndicated sludge. I'd met him a few times at parties, and he'd been useful to my P.R. men. I wandered over and said, 'Hello, Willie.'

He took both my hands. 'My dear, what luck. We can chat all the way to the lovely sunshine.'

Fur Face looked sick.

Look through the mist in Willie's gentian-blue eyes and something as shrewd and tough as a company accountant stared balefully out. He was rumoured to have three-quarters of a million that the tax-man had never seen. I kept my voice low.

'Willie, when we walk out of here keep close to me.'

'A pleasure, dearie.'

'Wrap it!' I said. 'Here's my boarding card. Put it flat on yours and slip the two to the stewardess. Then forget it—right?'

'Where will you be, love?'

'Not with you or the furry young man behind me.'

The mist had cleared completely, his voice was crisp. 'Not my type, dear—Fuzz?'

'Fuzz.'

'I'll collect when you're P.M.,' he said, and flipped the card into his pocket.

Lettcombe's man had no need to follow beyond the lounge. Short of hijacking the plane no one could get at me now. We shook hands and I contrived to get through the door with only Willie behind me. We passed three passages to ramps and at the fourth I stepped sideways and ran down to the boarding point. My flight wasn't full; by the time the stewardess got round to counting heads they'd be halfway over the Atlantic.

I tapped a harassed white-capped traffic man on the shoulder and complained I'd left my hand luggage behind with passport, money and tickets in it. He was used to fools; we were back in the main concourse in four minutes flat. I kept my head down as he waved me through control, then I pointed out the seat where I thought I'd left my bag, and, as he sped off, I stepped into a nearby gents ...

The address Kommer had given me turned out to be a bright, clean office up three flights of linoleumed stairs opposite Billingsgate fish market. A brass plate at street level said, 'Anglo-European Shipping: Import-Export.' It would have been difficult to get more ambiguous than that. I was in the office for six minutes and, when I stood on the pavement again, I wondered if I was making a fool of myself.

A bald-headed clerk had taken my scrap of paper, glanced at Kommer's signature, made out a form which he stamped and initialled, then turned away. I asked in some surprise if that was all.

'Well, I'd try and get down there by six,' he said. 'Get out to her on the ebb.'

'But what's the job?'

He looked puzzled and referred to a list on his desk. 'Deckhand.' He looked at my expensive suit. 'Got all your kit?'

I nodded.

'O.K., you won't need an advance then.' And that was that.

I weighed up whether to go on, then decided that, with Vashni safe, I could chance it. With an effort I overlaid the smelly prosaic activity of the market with a picture of the Ynysdeulleyn pub and Kommer's dreadful face. Was he just another blubbermouth—a bar-room bully? Every instinct told me no; then there were the villagers. My people are a secretive race but there had been more than that. There was something indefinably wrong with that whole community.

The revelation of Vashni had killed my original motive. Some shadow beings had dared to try and wipe out the inimitable Traherne, but, where before I had been coldly murderous about it, I now no longer gave a damn. What I hated was leaving a job half done, which was something hammered into me by my father. When I started something I couldn't rest until a double line had been finally drawn under it. I swung round on the pavement and collided with an irate fish porter.

'Mate,' he said, 'if you want two bleedin' stone of bleedin' cod dahn yer pretty clothes yer can muckin' well 'ave 'em!'

Queenboro' is a small improbable village jammed into a marshy corner on the north-west side of the Isle of Sheppey. I walked the half mile from the station lugging my newly acquired kit-bag, passed a glue works and a line of rotting hulks in a muddy creek, and came out on to a neat, safe little harbour. The pub where the office form directed me hung almost over the water. I dumped my bag down in the spotless bar and ordered a pint of bitter. I felt that a frayed blue jersey, seaman's trousers, and a wool hat was not sartorially correct for drinking Scotch. Again I felt doubts. The landlord was a bright, friendly man, a retired Trinity House pilot. Anything less sinister would be hard to imagine; the place exuded respectability.

I was on my second pint of warm bitter when a small bowler-hatted man bustled in. He didn't waste time.

'Traherne?'

I nodded.

'Finish your drink man; she's sailing in under the hour.'

The workmanlike, black-painted ship's tender wove out through a line of yachts and past the giant oil refinery on Grain Island. Massive tankers towered above us, big as office blocks. Out in the fairway we chugged past an interminable line of freighters muttering and tugging at their anchors like tethered circus elephants. When the tide turned they would trumpet irritably for pilots to take them up the London river.

One ship was a neat little coaster smelling as though she had recently carried timber. A scent of deep, still pinewoods, oddly out of place on the muddy Thames estuary. We sailed at once, dipping and bucking into the short vicious waves that are the speciality of those shallow waters. I'd covered most of this area two years ago in a ten-ton converted ketch belonging to an exalted personage who wanted a very private talk with me.

I ate a greasy dinner with a taciturn Swede who had cooked it, then sat on a winch in the stern watching the east coast vanish in the dark. No one came near me; if I was a deckhand I was on light duty. Eventually I climbed, fully clothed, into a narrow bunk in the fo'c'sle. Lying there I thought wryly that I was several kinds of bloody fool. No one knew where I was. There were twenty fathoms of cold North Sea water under me and it was a long long swim to shore. I drifted asleep and, as my mind stilled, Vashni came to me warm and happy.

A bright light shone in my eyes; I came awake and jack-knifed out of the bunk in one movement then dropped flat and swung stiffened closed legs in a vicious arc towards it. The overhead bulb lit and a frightened voice said, 'For Chrissake, man, what you at?' It was the Swede. 'Deckhand! Deckhand, my ass. Come on you're wanted.'

The deck was in darkness except for a single floodlight on a gangway rigged on the starboard side. Four men were grouped round it. I said, 'Fishing?' and no one answered. After a few minutes one of them shouted an order into the darkness and a searchlight beam bored down into the green depths of the sea. It was a strange exercise but I was no longer worried. This was outside the routine of any normal coaster.

A shadow wavered in the greenness below. Wavered and moved upward. A monstrous shape, huge, humped and black, stirring atavistic fears, prickling the hair on the nape of my neck. There was a roar of cascading water and compressed air and a submarine surfaced ten feet away. A superb piece of handling; the skipper must have had sublime confidence in his powers; one small mistake and both ships could have ended in a tangled mess of sinking steel. She edged closer. Someone shouted, 'Jump!' and I landed awkwardly on her wet deck. My bag dropped soggily beside me and I looked up into a sight from a Breugel painting of hell.

The coaster was invisible against a black wilderness of sea. A column of white light seemed to spring from the waves and, floating in it, was the gruesome head of Kommer.

'Welcome aboard, Minister,' he said.

I followed him down the conning tower and into a brightly lit area as full of pipes as a church organ. Half a dozen men stood quietly against banks of instruments.

Kommer snapped an order. A crewman ran up the conning tower ladder, hatches clanged, and the deck tilted slightly beneath our feet. Kommer said, 'North east by east.'

An elderly man in an officer's peak cap snapped, *'Ja Herr Kapitan,'* and backed politely out of our way as we walked aft.

Kommer's cabin was surprisingly spacious. I imagine he had a good deal more than his share of available space, for it was obviously not a large ship. I had made official tours of American atomic subs and, compared to this, their crews had room enough to contract agoraphobia; but Kommer did himself well. The furnishings were superb antiques and a thick Persian carpet covered the floor—it was a great deal better than my own Shiraz rugs. I sat in a Sheraton carver chair and sipped Glenlivet.

'You have eaten?'

I explained I'd done that on the coaster and his beautiful mouth twisted wryly.

'I apologize. Later we will give you something civilized.'

Once again the concentrated vitality of the man overlaid my fears. Ten minutes in his company and you forgot that hellish face.

I asked unnecessarily, 'You know who I am?'

'Of course. Your features may not be so ...' he paused, 'sensational as some, but you are well publicized.'

'You knew at Ynysdeullyn?'

'Naturally.'

'The job you offered was bait?'

'Not entirely,' he said.

One difficulty in dealing with him was the total lack of expression on that haphazard collection of features; the most wiley of poker players must give away some clue but here there was nothing. The pale eyes looked blankly at me.

'Mr Traherne,' he said, 'you have pushed your nose so far into my business that I either have to cut it right off or invite you right in.'

'You honestly think that I ...'

He held up a massive hand. 'I don't need sermons. Have you got where you are with the New Testament as a manual?'

It was not a comfortable thought but ... 'No,' I said slowly, 'I suppose not. I admit I'm not a candidate for canonization, but you know my position. Just what the hell do you think you could offer for me to compromise that?'

He peered at a nest of dials above his head, picked up a telephone and barked orders in German.

'Offer you?' he said. 'I can offer you two things: death in five minutes—or a quarter of a million pounds a year.'

73

He smiled sweetly. 'Tax free, Minister.'

I swallowed hard. There was no shadow of doubt that he meant what he said. His thought processes were not human. He was elemental—inevitable as the weather.

I said, 'Give me another drink—and tell me about it.'

It was a fantastic story. If I'd heard it from anyone else I would have laughed nervously and passed them on to the nearest psychiatrist. But Kommer dealt in cold facts. In the Hitler war he had been one of the last U-boat commanders to get a ship, and the youngest. At twenty-two he'd had eighteen months of command, collected every decoration the Third Reich could lavish on him, and sunk an incredible tonnage of Allied shipping. Once, he boarded a Russian destroyer off its own coast and fought its crew to a standstill; then he shelled its base with its own guns and scuttled it. For that Hitler invented a special order. I asked what happened to the captured crew. As far as he could show emotion he looked astonished.

'Happened? They died. What would I do with prisoners on an *unterseeboot*?'

When his country was near capitulation he sank his ship and took his crew ashore as civilians. He was a bit vague about the next few months, but I gathered his method was to infiltrate his pirates into a town being overrun by the Allies, then, when the disorganization was at its height, they would carry out a carefully planned scheme of looting. When the surrender came he had three of his men left—they were still with him—and enough portable treasure to set him up as a respectable ship-owner. He soon tired of that and took to large-scale dope smuggling. He had a direct route from Indo-China to London; then the French débâcle upset his lines of supply.

The skipper of one of his Bombay-based ships had worked up a lucrative sideline in illegal immigrants. When Kommer discovered it he put the fear of hell into the man and developed the trade; then the going got tough as one by one the holes on the English south coast were plugged.

Five years ago he heard that the West German government was scrapping a quantity of mothballed armaments left over from the war. Among them was a U-boat, almost completed when disaster hit the shipyards thirty years before. It cost him a lot of money to buy and three times as much more to persuade the original makers to complete the job. By the time she was afloat he was a comparatively poor man.

He talked his Board of Trade into granting a licence and set her up in Hamburg as a tourist attraction—visits aboard—short expensive trips out into the North Sea. She had everything but armaments, and he built in an observation panel forward. The converted torpedo room could hold thirty tourists in comfort. It could also hold eighty immigrants in a very fair imitation of hell. Averaging four trips a month and charging three hundred pounds per immigrant he grossed an incredible million plus a year; and he was uncatchable. With his Hamburg registration he had a perfect right to be at sea, and with that vessel, landing his cargoes unseen was child's play.

When he finished I found I had been so engrossed my

full glass was still clutched in my hand. He was genuinely concerned. 'Ah, you must not drink that, Minister,' he said. 'It will be warm.'

As he took the glass I asked, 'What happens if you're ever really caught. Suppose your own navy, for instance, want to inspect?'

He poured water on to the new drink. 'We dive,' he said. 'We have not seen their signals and we dive.'

'But suppose they chase you. You can't outrun the equipment they carry nowadays.'

'What problem?' he asked. 'There are the tubes.'

I didn't follow him and must have shown it.

'The torpedo tubes,' he said impatiently. 'Everything works. A weighted body can be shot out and not surface for weeks.' He chuckled. 'I have what you call true German efficiency—I carry a special ballast of iron bars. Then I surface and I have a clean ship.'

It was impossible to feel anger. Horror yes, but you don't get angry with the elements or scream curses at the hurricane that smashes a town. At the time, my feelings centred on myself—with what I now knew I was a dead man. Kommer was thumbing over a ledger he had taken from a wall safe.

'You will want to see figures,' he said. 'No one should join a business until he has seen the books.'

He was perfectly serious and that simple action did more to frighten me than anything that had gone before. My nerves were screaming. He had a full house and knew every card in my hand. It didn't occur to him that I could do other than accept. When I spoke my voice was steady. Bluff was the essence of the game.

'I can't see why I am worth so much to you,' I said. 'If I were in your place I'd kill me off.'

'Kill you!' He sounded really shocked. 'My dear Minister, with you on our Board we cannot lose. You will soon be in such a position politically you can cover us whatever happens. Make a few trips with us now; have your share placed in a Geneva bank, and then go back to your work. You will continue to collect your share, but you will not be called on for such work again.'

I saw what he meant. I should be hopelessly compromised and I could rely on him to provide enough evidence for my enemies to blow my whole party apart if I failed him. That vast skull housed a brain like Napoleon.

'Very well, Captain,' I said. 'When do we start?'

We docked in Hamburg at lunchtime the next day. Kommer was in towering good spirits and showed me the entire ship. He was very proud of her. The discipline was of the old German Navy and the crew came automatically to attention as he passed. There were ten of them; they wore a uniform very like the Navy and there was no sloppiness. The three officers were older men and could have passed an admiral's inspection.

The language used was German. I knew enough of it to understand the orders, but there was very little talking. Kommer was not merely a disciplinarian; he could run men like machines, command absolute obedience in any situation. I stood with him on the tiny bridge as we cruised up the river to our dock. Having decided I was with him, he held little back.

The immigrants were flown into Frankfurt. There was an organization in India to collect them and they paid the full fare before they left. The total cost per head was around five thousand pounds and the organization was quite happy to advance the money. Once they were in England it was collected, with interest, by instalments. Every large town had agents, and, as Lettcombe had said, it was wise to settle. The immigrant was rarely touched since he was the potential earner, but they all had families in India. I gathered that the Indian hard men were something very special indeed.

The next move was to shift the immigrant batches from the airfield to various hideouts on the European west coast. One of these was a holiday camp in Holland. They all had some sort of papers and if they were kept on the move the local authorities didn't bother with them. When a batch was ready Kommer was notified of the pick-up point. The only thing he was reticent about was landing points on the English side, however it looked as though I'd soon be finding that out for myself. What amazed me was the sheer size of the operation. Kommer was an essential part, but was he the king pin? It was difficult to think of him working under others, but not impossible. The thing was a company, with a board of directors—was he chairman? When I had, for instance, asked him why he had tried to kill me in London, he said shortly that the attempts were not by his orders.

We spent a week in the Hamburg dock, and I took my turn showing the public over the ship. They paid ten deutchmarks for the tour and we averaged about a hundred a day. It was a pleasant handful of chicken feed for the crew. I soon noticed that to be alone I needed to be in the lavatory or my tiny cabin next to Kommer, and I never left the ship. I tried once and two of the young crew members stood stolidly at the end of the gangway, one of them cleaning his nails thoughtfully with a flick knife. If there were English or Americans among the tourists I joined in the commentary but my companion was always one of the English-speaking members of the crew.

Kommer vanished for two days, and, when he came back, called me into his cabin and gave me details of the coming run. The pick-up point was a small village near Flushing in Holland, and he traced our route down through the Channel. When the red pencil turned north round Land's End I thanked God I'd got Vashni out of it. I knew now where we were heading.

Living with Kommer was rather like setting up house with a jovial tiger. He enjoyed life enormously. He absorbed food, drink, and work in quantites that would have taxed the capacity of three normal men. He took constant exercise to absorb his fantastic energy, skipping, and pounding a punching bag for hours on end. When he found I could almost wrestle against him if he tied his right hand to his side, nothing was too good for me.

He was very well educated. His cabin was lined with books. He could talk art and literature and politics, and his ideas weren't warmed-over hashes of what he had read; but he had strange blind spots. He could not, for instance, distinguish one musical note from another. One wet afternoon I tried him on Jung. The effect was curious: he immediately became restless and irritable.

I switched to Bertrand Russell and from there it wasn't far to comparative religion and ethics. I thought he was rather silent and when I looked round he was asleep, sprawled vastly across his desk. He never slept in the daytime. I could only think that this strange mind had unconsciously sealed itself against anything that involved it with the normal mores of humanity. At dinner on the night before we sailed, he paused for a moment in stuffing great gobbets of near raw steak through those delicate rosebud lips, and asked, 'Do you know Hamburg?'

I answered rather bitterly that I hadn't had a chance to see it.

'Come, my friend,' he roared. 'We will enjoy ourselves.'

At four in the morning I was back on the ship fighting against waves of nausea. The variations of human sexual conduct have never been of interest to me; but Hamburg's night life provided food for thought and I had learned a good deal more about Kommer. I could hear him blundering about in his cabin next door, and I wanted very much to be somewhere else; somewhere a long, long way away. When I thought of what I had just done to him I sweated.

Two points stood out in that long, fuddled night. At the door of one back-street club, two burly chuckers out decided Kommer was not a member. He was very reasonable and offered them a fistful of notes. God knows why, but they refused it and tried to hustle him out of the doorway; perhaps the police had been sorting the place out. Kommer put his money away, wrapped an arm lovingly round each and squeezed.

A man screaming is a horrible noise; a man screaming

like a woman is an obscenity. I beat the great shoulders with my clenched fists until he dropped the men in the gutter. As we drove off I could see them writhing on the pavement like damaged insects.

A couple of places later we were jammed in a tiny foetid theatre that felt as though it were a mile underground. Four bored girls were performing lesbian tricks on a minute stage. Their movements were real and explicit enough but the effect was pure tedium. Kommer watched for five minutes then walked on to the stage, tucked one of the girls under his arm and vanished into the wings.

Two of the younger crew members were with us; they had drunk nothing all evening; now they stood quietly on each side of the stage, hands casually slipped into their jackets. No one interfered. The room was hot and smelly and had gone very quiet, and the noises off were not pleasant. After a while Kommer sauntered back into the lights, yawned and looked speculatively at the remaining dancers. As they scuttled off he roared with gigantic laughter and lumbered to the bar at the rear of the auditorium. The audience sighed with relief and an indifferent comedian came on nervously telling obscene elephant jokes that must have originated in Hannibal's army.

Half an hour later one of the lesbian girls was hurried out towards the exit between two women. She was wrapped in a heavy coat, her feet dragged and she was moaning continuously. As she passed Kommer she screamed and struggled feebly. I had drunk a great deal of bad liquor but I was suddenly cold sober. The taller of the women came back and said in English, 'God, I need a drink.' I bought her one. She didn't comment on what had happened but it was a good ten minutes before she remembered what she was there for and suggested we went upstairs. I thought quickly, then shouted across to Kommer, 'I'll be back in a minute.'

The cold eyes flicked over the woman. 'Kurt will go with you,' he said. He had drunk enough to kill a man and in that instant he was sober enough to have piloted his ship.

Kurt at least had the decency to stay outside. The girl was from Lancashire and didn't believe in an oblique approach. I had hardly shut the door before she was sprawled naked on the divan bed. I sat beside her and asked, 'Do you want to earn some money?'

She closed her plump thighs and sat up. 'What a bloody silly question. What d'you think I do? Give it away to the Salvation Army?'

I whispered, 'Keep your voice down. Was that girl you helped a friend?'

She nodded.

'I want you to do something for me. I'll give you twenty English pounds and what you do will fix that big bastard downstairs—right?'

'Do you know what he did to Thelma?' she asked.

I said I could guess.

'You wouldn't,' she said. 'No one could. He's not human.' Her breath came in a near sob. 'And she never had a man in her life; being near men made her sick.'

I got out a pen and found I had nothing to write on. She crossed to a chest of drawers in a corner, her white bottom flicking as she moved. She was still under thirty and attractive enough, but my body didn't stir. Vashni was all I had of that and all I would ever have. Thinking of her in that place seemed obscene.

The girl gave me a pad. I covered three pages, scraping my mind for remembered detail, then sealed them in an envelope and gave it to her. It was for Lettcombe but I addressed it to the British Embassy; I wasn't going to trust the post with that particular piece of dynamite.

'I'm not going near the bloody Fuzz,' she said quickly.

'You don't have to, get the address from the phone book and go and deliver it.'

I gave her money and went out with my coat over my arm. Kurt stared impassively through the open door as she sat naked on the bed, then followed me down to the bar.

We slipped down river on the afternoon ebb. A cheerful customs man called, 'Going smuggling again, *Herr Kapitan*?'

Kommer shouted an unprintable joke about a mermaid's brothel and we were through the lock gates. We cruised on the surface. At vast expense Kommer had fitted very modern diesels and, once out of the river, he must have averaged eighteen knots. The endless duned façade of the Frisian Islands streamed past our starboard side; long before it was dark I'd had enough and went below to my bunk. After the previous night's entertainment I was tired to my marrow and I drifted asleep to the rhythmic thud of Kommer's great hands as he smashed the punch bag in the passage outside.

The sickening roll of the ship woke me. A dim blue

emergency lamp glowed in its cage. I glanced at my watch—4.30; I had slept for over seven hours and I was ravenously hungry. The corridor and control room were deserted. From the motion we must be lying at anchor in shallow water.

I had one hand on the conning tower ladder when the thought struck me that here was a chance I should never get again. Kommer's door was open. I slipped into the cabin, switched on the light, and looked at the desk. It was almost a certainty that anything interesting would be out of my reach in the safe, but it was worth a try. Or was it? Anyone entering a tiger's den without checking if he were at home deserved all he got. I thought of what I should get and shivered. There were five drawers: four yielded ships routine—port clearances, maintenance checks, supply records and accounts. I moved only the corners of the papers with my finger tips. They were clipped in meticulous squared piles. When a drop of sweat fell on a receipt for thirty gallons of lubricating oil, I stopped, stood upright, and forced myself to take ten deep breaths.

I had never met a human being who could frighten me or put me in awe. I reasoned it out when I was fighting boys twice my age on the Brynmawr mountainside. A man was a sack of skin containing a certain quantity of meat, guts, and blood. If he were a king, a drunk, or a saint he still had to perform his natural functions. Physically he was vulnerable—you just had to find out how. As I grew I applied the method to mental power and found it still worked. It didn't work for Kommer. The thought of being found with my hand in his private trough left me weak. I finished the breathing exercise and opened the last drawer.

Guns are something I've never taken an interest in. The one in the top of the drawer was big enough to interest the Royal Artillery and it had an eight-inch barrel with a curious bulbous attachment on the muzzle end. Under it was a note book; I would imagine it held a great deal I would have liked to know, but though I can read German very slowly if I concentrate hard, I could never decipher two consecutive words of Gothic script. I edged the book back under the portable cannon then noticed a roll of typewritten sheets beside it.

Ten sheets of quarto close typed, can hold a lot of names. They were all Indian or Pakistani, Singh predominated but, by the look of the rest, there was a fair cross-section of the whole Sub-Continent. There was a cross or tick against each name. The ticks outnumbered the crosses by about four to one. By now, even standing in the current of cold air sweeping through the deserted ship, I felt as though I'd stepped under a shower with my clothes on. I laid the first sheet carefully back in the drawer and a name stood out like a neon sign. CHOTA DAL.

A voice echoed in the tower and boots thumped down the ladder. My heart changed smoothly into overdrive. I slid the papers in beside the gun and closed the drawer. There was no point in trying to get out. When Kommer came in I was sitting on the desk slopping Glenlivet into a glass; he trudged over, took the bottle from me and poured half a tumbler for himself.

'You need a drink, my friend?' he asked amiably.

'Always when you wish help yourself. Come, we load the cargo.'

The ship was moored between two large broad-beamed motor cruisers, their rope fenders grinding against her flanks. The forward hatch was open and, outlined in faint blue light, a stream of silent people carrying cases and bundles picked a hesitant passage over the gangways and clambered out of sight into the bowels of the sub. The loading took twenty minutes; except for a muttered word or two no one spoke. Once a baby cried, the officer checking a list stepped forward and the mother muffled it in her shawl.

I am a natural sailor but by the time the hatch was closed I'd had enough of the pig-like wallowing the ship was indulging herself in. The thought of what it must be like in the torpedo room didn't improve my stomach. When we got under way I stayed on the bridge with the duty officer. The sea soon smoothed to long sweeping rollers coming out of the north behind us with a crisp of white foam on their crests. When the night air had blown my head clear I went below.

The steel door to the forward compartment was clamped shut, and I imagined eighty frightened people crouched in there. The cook came out into the control room and shouted that food was ready; meals were taken at odd times and were always full scale. Kommer was already in the mess room eating steadily. He liked to have a lot of food in front him at once and used a huge Georgian pewter dish. He waved a hand and pushed a bottle of excellent Burgundy towards me.

The food was the same for the whole crew and it was

at the standard of an internationally famous restaurant. The galley was a gem of planning and space saving, and God knows from what gastronomic eminence Kommer had seduced his chef.

I jerked my head forward. 'How do they eat?'

'Uh?' Kommer wiped his mouth delicately. 'Oh, they bring food—rice—their own stuff.'

'What do they do for sanitation?'

He laughed. 'Don't worry, Minister. You won't have to clean ship. The crew get a bonus.' He dug a fork down into his dish. 'They have buckets.' It was sensible of course. It had taken me several minutes to work out the complications of a pressurized water closet. The passengers would have flooded the ship at the first try.

'How long will we be at sea?' I tried to sound casual.

'Thirty-six hours. You can get some sleep—it is a long time since you had a party like Hamburg eh?'

I took the rest of the Burgundy to my cabin. I needed something to damp down my mind. The hatch of the torpedo room would be shut for the next day and a half. On the surface the air-conditioners might just keep the atmosphere breathable. What happened when we dived? There was at least one child aboard. An anger I had not felt before started to burn inside me.

In that steel womb time was meaningless. We ate four more superb meals. In the daylight hours I occasionally went up to the bridge, but visibility stayed down to twenty yards as we ploughed through drizzling rain. The seaways of the English Channel are crowded as Piccadilly Circus in rush hour. Whenever the weather lifted for a moment there were always several vessels in sight, but it is doubtful if they saw our half-submerged whale-back. I was practising my German on the radio operator when his set came alive with an angry stutter of morse; he waved to me to be quiet, jotted something down on his pad and called urgently, *'Herr Leutenant!'*

The oldest of the officers glanced at the message, shouted for Kommer and jabbed his thumb on a red button. Alarm bells hammered through the ship; the crew moved with a smooth efficient rush, and by the time Kommer lumbered from his cabin we were diving steeply, loose objects clattering forward along the deck. Even through four inches of steel bulkhead I heard the terrified wail that came from the torpedo room.

Kommer stood beside me tapping his fingers on the depth gauge. The minutes passed as the needle edged round the dial. At thirty fathoms he moved his hand horizontally, the helmsman spun a wheel and the deck levelled under our feet. I raised my eyebrows.

'Navy,' he said. 'Your navy. They are not polite—they did not enquire for recognition.' He passed the crumpled message to me and I deciphered it slowly.

'HEAVE TO IMMEDIATELY—REPEAT IMMEDIATELY—FOR BOARDING.'

The first explosion came an hour later. There must have been some very worried men up above to make that decision. Kommer's little eyes did not even blink. He cocked his great head to one side; one professional judging another. 'A loose pattern,' he said conversationally. 'But he does not wish to hit us; we will show him what an old fox can do.'

He took the wheel, cut his motors and handled the ship

like a glider, swooping and hovering in eerie silence, but always falling. He brought her to rest at last with an almost imperceptible bump, said, 'Mud and sand; we stay here.' Then very gently, 'I think you have betrayed me, Mr Traherne, but we are safe enough with you aboard.'

I tried to sound astonished. 'What the hell d'you mean? What chance have I had to ... ?'

He crossed to the chart table and dabbed a finger like a brown banana down on to it. 'We are here. Why would the Navy be here? No one comes here.'

I was trying to keep my voice level. 'An exercise: you ran into them by chance, they probably think you're a Russian.'

He didn't bother to answer. The whole ship was silent and the air was becoming very thick. He looked at his watch. 'I am paid for live cargo. Switch on engines.'

As the electric motors whined into life the room filled with a rhythmic thudding roar from the hydrophone amplifiers.

Kommer barked, 'Stop engines.'

The ship sank slowly, then the lights flickered and she rolled ponderously to one side as the depth-charges clanged and clawed at the eardrums. We settled again on the bottom, this time with an ominous crunch.

I said, 'You might as well go up. They know I am aboard but I told them to forget it.'

'So? You are a hero?' He sounded amused. 'Then we must persuade them another way to stop throwing things at me.'

He snapped an order. Two crew men grabbed my arms

and expertly lashed my wrists. Two more took up positions by the torpedo room door, clutching short rubber truncheons in their right hands. The elderly officer spun the clamps and the door burst open. An unbelievable stench rushed out, an almost solid compound of waste products, exhausted air and pure animal fear.

A wave of brown bodies hurled itself at the doorway, three more of the crew fought them back while Kommer shoving me ahead, ducked into the room. The long-barrelled pistol was in his hand as the frantic Indians rushed him and he swatted them aside like insects until they crouched moaning at his feet in petrified heaps.

It is impossible to describe the condition of that room and I am not going to try. Looking at it I forgot the danger of the ships overhead until a faint concussion pulsed at the eardrums. They were still searching. Then something happened so quickly I had no time to absorb it logically. Kommer pointed the gun at a man lying against the near bulkhead. Two crew members seized him, slammed back a circular hatch, thrust him in and closed it.

Kommer shouted back into the control room, 'Fire one!'

There was a hiss of compressed air and he called, 'Start engines!' He ducked back through the doorway and said, 'The quarters here are not so luxurious, Minister, but make yourself at home.'

I spoke in a horrified whisper, 'You bloody murderer! That man ...' I pointed a shaking finger at the tube.

'That man will have surfaced by now,' he said. 'It's just possible he will be alive; but either way he will be an excellent messenger, and if that doesn't convince them they must leave me alone they can have some more.'

The door slammed behind him and I heard the bars being hammered into place.

A voice behind me said, 'I'd better untie your wrists, darling.'

CHAPTER FIVE

Strangely, my first reaction was anger. As Vashni cut the rope I turned, gripped her arms, and snarled, 'You bloody little fool. How the devil did you manage to get into this mess?'

It is difficult for a European to imagine the mental suffering of those eighty odd people crammed into that vile sardine can. Most of them were country people from small villages. The nearest they had been to modern technology was a rare visit by officials and doctors in battered cars. They must inevitably by now have been mad with fear and in the last stages of adrenalin exhaustion. A ritualistically clean people, they lay in their own filth. A people whose eating and natural functions were governed by meticulous observances of caste, they were crammed together in a wild confusion of limbs; yet defeated and beaten down to the basic level of survival, they swept terror aside and rose against me. A wall of furious brown faces hemmed me in, and a ragged little man whose filthy turban reached to my shoulder, hissed through gapped and broken teeth, 'Take your hands from the Honoured One, dog's dung, or we will kill you.'

Vashni spoke six words. The ring broke, and with both hands to their foreheads, the people backed away; then she put her hands together, bowed her head in submission and whispered, 'Beat me.'

It was so exactly what I felt like doing that, for a

moment, I was startled; then I put my arms round her and roared with laughter. It was the best thing I could have done. Something was needed to bring sanity back into that hell-hole and by chance I had hit on it. They laughed with me, rolling around the steel deck holding their sides. It was mostly hysteria and they quietened at a word from Vashni, but the animal fear had gone and they were human again.

Vashni had told them I was her husband. From then on they treated me with exaggerated respect—but they wouldn't face her without the ritual gesture of worship; and, even in that crammed space, they contrived to leave a small clear circle round her.

The ship was moving. The beat of her engines like another heart in the body. The air was stifling but breathable and, as always happens, the nose and throat eventually accustomed themselves even to that complicated stench. It was some time before I realized it was the diesels I could hear and we must have surfaced.

Vashni pressed herself close to me, pouring out her story. We had both double-crossed each other. As soon as she thought I was on a plane and safely out of the country, she went off to Larri's clinic and put round the word that she wanted to see a new arrival. Within an hour she had met one of Lettcombe's five immigrants. He had a resident's permit in his pocket and felt secure enough to talk. After that it was simple enough to infiltrate the route. What puzzled me was why, after being content to tail along in Larri's wake, she now tore on to the trail like an infuriated tigress. I turned her face towards me and she said, 'I *had* to stop them—they tried to kill you.' Her voice held wonder that anyone could contemplate such unspeakable blasphemy.

Larri, of course, thought she was leaving for India and he was obviously as relieved as I to know she would be safely out of the way. He had seen her to the air terminal and gone off back to the ambiguous atmosphere of Ynysdeullyn. She then took a Frankfurt plane, changed into a sari and sat in the arrival lounge waiting for large parties of Indians to come through. It took three days and several false starts until she got results. Her technique was simply to join up with a likely party and ask a few idle questions. Once, she got as far as a hospital staff quarters before she realized she was with a collection of earnest doctors attending a conference.

When she hit the right lot no one bothered her. A brisk Dutch couple met them and whisked them on to a train for a holiday camp in Holland; they were well fed and the camp was clean. It was a very mixed party: some were breadline poor, but some carried a remarkable amount of portable wealth. No one realized the hell of the next stage to come.

When she finished I said, 'Look, aren't you supposed to obey me?'

'I'm sorry, darling,' she said quickly.

I was still angry. 'You'll be sorrier if you try anything like this again. I'll tan that elegant bottom of yours until you sleep on your face for a month.'

She smiled, then suddenly her mood changed. 'But I told you,' she said urgently, 'I *had* to do it. You will never be safe until these people are caught.'

And that bothered me very much. She had known what

94

was going on for a long time. She loved her people and hated the hardships the racket was causing them, but it had taken the revelation on the floor of my living-room and a night in my bed to bring her to the point where she would give her life for them; and it wasn't for them— it was for me. If I told her that stepping in front of an express train was necessary to my well-being she would do it calmly and without a second thought. The idea was utterly alien to me: I had never had that for anyone— or had I?

I thought about my own cherished image. The tough Welshman. Hard, unscrupulous, born to fight his way from poverty to power. That little bit of libido had done very well for me; and how exactly was it to fit in with what I had just realized—that I would beat her to the express train by several lengths if it was necessary to her happiness? I tilted her face up and kissed her; her mouth opened and clung wetly to mine and the problem melted in the taste of her tongue. When we surfaced I noticed everyone was looking studiously in another direction.

A woman shuffled forward on her knees and offered a plastic plate of cold saffron rice. Vashni touched her forehead and took the plate. The woman put her hands together and pressed her head to the cold steel of the deck. In that place my stomach heaved at the sight of food, but Vashni ate the mess slowly and carefully with her fingers. The whole incident disturbed me. I looked down at the woman and she had not moved.

'Why?' I asked.

Vashni said nervously, 'Darling, she's just being respectful and kind, she ...' Her voice faltered then she said firmly, 'No, I must not lie to you, but you must try to understand. I'm a perfectly ordinary woman, but I am, just because I was born into it, a priestess of Dûrga.'

'Who's that?'

'It's very complicated. You can't learn about Hinduism in five minutes. Very, very simply she is the Mother.'

'A Goddess?'

'Oh yes. She is another aspect of Kali Ma—the Black Mother. She is the Creator, Kali the Destroyer.' Her voice was thoughtful. 'They are the same thing really you know.'

I didn't know and I didn't like this at all.

'What you're saying is that you're some sort of holy person, like a nun?' I hoped I had kept my voice casual.

'Oh worse than that, darling.' She spoke gravely, but her eyes were amused. 'When I'm at home I have to serve in the temple once or twice a year—only at great festivals like Dussehra—but when I'm not doing that I *am* Dûrga. I told you it was complicated.'

'That's all I need,' I said bitterly. 'The Party is going to love an Indian Goddess for a leader's wife; and what does that do for me? I suppose it's sacrilege every time I have you?'

'Just the opposite,' she said. 'You people really are a barbaric lot. Now with us, love-making has great religious virtue.'

'Consider me a convert,' I said.

Out of the corner of my eye I saw the door move. There was just time to get away from her as it clanged open and, when Kommer came in, I was among a group on the other side of the room. Vashni's face was covered by her sari.

Kommer jerked his head. 'All right, outside, Traherne.'

I was no longer a guest. He shoved me roughly through the control room and into his cabin. As he closed the door, he smashed the back of a hand contemptuously into my face. I saw it coming, ducked and caught the blow on the top of my head, but even so, when the firework display stopped, I was sprawled on my back across his desk with the great bladder face staring impassively down at me.

'Do they know you are aboard?' he demanded.

My head ached vilely, but somehow I had to keep him guessing and stay alive.

'Of course they do. Why in hell did you have to do that?' I grumbled.

It was a deadly game. One wrong card and I lost more than my life. Whatever he did to me he must not suspect that Vashni was among the cargo. I sat up very cautiously.

'No,' he said. 'I do not think they know you are here. They would not dare to depth charge me if they knew that.'

He slopped a drink into a glass and I watched as he sipped appreciatively. I needed one very badly indeed but I was damned if I would ask.

'What use are you?' he demanded. 'No use as a hostage, no use as a partner.'

I had printed the message to Lettcombe and not signed it. He needed a lead very badly and I was pretty sure he would take action even without my name on it. I don't really know why I did that. A Celtic love of the devious perhaps; but I think, at the time, I had achieved a sense of freedom, and after years of limelight, I was my own man again. Frankly, if I'd thought of depth-charges I wouldn't have been so damned clever. I stared straight up into the cold pebble eyes.

'Kommer,' I said, 'I'm as fond of my own skin as the next man; do you honestly think I'd be here without backing?'

He made an impatient gesture and I hurried on, 'Think about it, man, and you'll see I'm telling the truth. The whole operation was planned from London. You don't stand a chance. Run me into the nearest port and I'll see you're only charged with attempting to land illegal immigrants.'

The rose-bud mouth smiled sweetly. 'And the man from the tube? They will think he was practising underwater swimming, eh?'

I shrugged. 'He panicked and used the escape hatch incorrectly.'

He reached slowly towards me with his free hand. I wondered dully if it was worth fighting; I might as well have taken on a bulldozer with boxing gloves, but I couldn't let myself go down without a try. The great fleshy fingers were within inches of my throat. I thought wearily, 'All right, boyo, here it is,' and I felt nothing but a hope that he'd get it over quickly and a vast sadness that I would never be with Vashni again. The hand came on, picked up the whisky bottle and tossed it to me; then he roared with laughter as I caught it awkwardly and reached past him for a glass.

'Damn you to hell, Traherne,' he chuckled. 'I like you. Doesn't anything scare you?'

'I'm a rabbit—but a political one.'

'Rabbit!'

He turned to the door and was still chuckling when

I hit him with the bottle. A bottle of Scotch contains forty fluid ounces, and the bottle itself weighs around a pound and a half. Most of the Scotch was still there and I hit him squarely over the gleaming crown of his head with my full strength. It was a murderous blow and if the danger to Vashni hadn't blotted out all other thought I couldn't have done it even to him.

He turned, and for once the scattered features showed surprise, then he toppled like a dynamited chimney. He fell on me, and as the light flickered out in those stony eyes a hand gripped my thigh. I smothered a scream—a few feet away crew members would be sitting round the mess table. The hand tightened; fire burned through my flesh and licked along the thigh bone. My head swam; every toe of my right foot was an incandescent flame. I scrabbled from under him and struck wildly at the great calm face. The fingers loosened but I had to tear each one separately from my leg, blood oozing after them through the cloth of my trousers.

Somehow I had to stand. I clawed upright, bringing down a shower of beautifully bound books from the packed shelves. It was strange; my immediate instinct was to put them tidily back, but if I had stooped then, I should have been down again for good. I pulled open the desk drawer and found his gun. There was no point in waiting, at any moment some crew member could knock on the door; then the phone rang. The sudden clamour left me sweating and trembling but I picked the receiver up and barked, *'Kapitan hier.'*

'Kapitan. Stevern Sie jetzt! Die küste ist nahe.' The voice sounded worried.

I growled, *'Ja. Ich Komm,'* and put the instrument gently down.

The door of the mess room was mercifully closed. Life was coming back painfully to my numbed leg and I somehow shuffled the few steps to the control room. There were six of them in there. The wireless operator saw me first and his shout startled me; my finger closed on the trigger and a bullet smashed into the instrument beside him. It was the best thing I could have done; the six froze, and I didn't blame them. Even when I shouldered the door to behind me and dropped the locking bar they continued giving excellent imitations of plaster saints. They were so fascinated by the business end of Kommer's formidable artillery that I had to shout twice before I could get two of them to unseal the torpedo room.

Again that fearsome stench rolled out, but this time there was no one to stem the human flood. I climbed a few steps of the conning tower ladder and looked frantically round for Vashni. For one heart-stopping moment I thought she was down under the trampling feet, then she was thrust up out of the mêlée by two burly, black-bearded Indians. I got an arm round her and lugged her up the ladder into air that tasted sweet as honey.

The ship was nosing along a coastline of red cliffs. At their foot a great stretch of white sand flowed seaward. Filthy air and a noise like a catfight streamed up the funnel of the tower. Hands clawed at the ladder and the white contorted face of a crew member came level with the deck; I smashed a toe into his mouth and as he fell the decibels from below increased. I swung the hatch shut and the sound sank to a murmur.

Vashni twisted her hands together. 'The people; we must help the people.'

'I'm a thought busy for welfare work, *cariad*,' I said. 'How's your swimming?'

She looked blankly at me. I spoke slowly and clearly, 'Get down the outside ladder and stand on the main deck.'

She said, 'Yes, Tomas,' and swung over the rail.

Something decisive had happened below, for the noise had stopped. I was in no position to know which side had won but, whoever it was, they wanted fresh air. The hatch heaved and jerked beneath me. I gave Vashni sixty carefully counted seconds then jumped. The body of the ship was ten feet below. I landed on the leg Kommer had gripped; Vashni caught me and while I cursed steadily in Welsh, pain flowed round the bruised tendons. A grey splash appeared on the wet deck at my feet, and a high shrieking whine died away over the sea leaping back from the echoing cliff.

For one appalled second I stared up at a figure that would have made the day for the most conscientious of horror film directors. Incredibly, Kommer was alive, the vast torso squeezing up through the hatch like an obscene worm, the head no longer remotely human—a painted beach ball gaily striped in moving bands of scarlet. Vashni screamed; I wrapped one arm round her and dived into the calm muddy water.

Had the ship been travelling at more than a few knots the twin screws must have had us. The insinuating tug of their vortices drew us steadily down, something very solid smashed into the heel of my left shoe, then the steady pulse of engines was swallowed in the sea.

The sensible course was to stay under until my breath gave out, but Vashni was limp against me and there's healthier stuff for lungs than the cold waters of St Brides Bay. I knew exactly where we were. In my short-trousered Welsh schooldays, the chapels of Brynmawr ceased once a year from consigning each other's congregations to fire and brimstone and organized an ecumenical outing for the offspring of the faithful. Any child who had memorized a hundred lines of the Old Testament and could give a reasonably coherent account of one of its formidable heroes, became a member of the elect and could board the bus for the salty heaven of Newgale sands. Elisha earned me many a sunburned backside and sticky length of genuine Welsh candy—Cymru woven into the sucked centre and Birmingham on the wrapper. I've had an irrational liking for bears all my adult life.

When we surfaced I trod water holding Vashni's head clear of the small waves, waiting for the distant engine note to change, and the sleek sea Juggernaut to rush down upon us; but the sound grew fainter, the blood beat of the engines leached from my body. A gull swooped out of the blue sky-blaze, braked in mid air, saw me move, and flapped disappointed away.

Vashni said, 'Darling, I can't swim a stroke so I'm keeping still; is that right?'

'What the hell did they teach you at that expensive school then?' I asked, and turned her on her back.

We were no more than half a mile out. Kommer must have known those waters like a Skomer sea-gull; there couldn't have been two feet between his keel and the sand—nothing could have followed him in here. By the sun it was around six a.m. when I hauled out on the beach feeling like a dyspeptic sea-lion. Vashni had lain calmly and uncomplainingly in the water as I lugged her along. Once, I spared breath to ask if she was all right, and she said, 'Of course, darling, you're here.'

I thought sourly that such sublime confidence was going to take some living up to. We had come ashore at a point where the main road swoops down almost into the sea and the four-mile stretch of sand was empty. The inn opposite looked as though its occupants had been dead for a year; I thought of beating on the peeling paint of the front-door, but decided against it and tramped soggily north, Vashni trailing a few paces behind.

I don't know what the driver of the milk lorry thought of us. I stopped him by standing in the middle of the road, and, before he could speak, pressed a wet fiver into his hand. It is a slander on the Welsh to call us avaricious but our non-conformist God has never been over-generous and we don't refuse manna when it drops. If my father had been Lloyd George we couldn't have been more tenderly treated. Our driver promptly abandoned his round and a quarter of an hour later jammed on his brakes outside a cottage in St David's. The milk on the back had probably churned to cheese, but he handed Vashni over to his wife who clucked off upstairs with her while we walked round the corner to find his brother.

Twenty years can be expected to change people and towns. When I was last here, St David's had seemed nothing but the vast austerity of the cathedral, lightly ringed by a sleepy village. Getting transport to cover the forty odd miles to Ynysdeullyn would have been a major undertaking. Our lorry driver's brother owned a garage with the type of forecourt that is international ground from Texas to Timbuktu; and the town, though still beautiful, had been changed by the yearly tourist harvest until that subtly overshadowed its ancient reason for being. Another damp currency note produced a vast modern limousine and we walked in on Larri as he was sitting down to breakfast.

When he saw us he waved a nonchalant hand, grabbed the remaining pieces of toast and said smugly, 'I'm afraid all the breakfast has gone.'

'Don't you even want to know why we're here?' Vashni asked crossly.

'I have quite enough difficulty knowing why *I* am here at this time of day without worrying about other people's geographical position.' He smiled. 'But you do seem to have been extraordinarily careless. What did you do; fall asleep on your planes and circumnavigate the globe?'

Dawa Chand fussed round feeding us while we brought Larri up to date, and, as we talked, his flippancy vanished.

At last he said, 'I think you have both been incredibly lucky and quite incredibly foolish. I tried to get you safely out of the way, but since you seem determined to shove your necks under the chopper, you'd better do it my way.'

He crossed to the window, speaking without taking his eyes from the turquoise flash of the sea.

'All right. This Kommer is out under there somewhere. From what you tell me, he's badly hurt and his cargo may have taken over the ship. If he's still in charge he'll run—if he's not, my untutored countrymen have probably wrecked the sub. Either way we shouldn't be bothered by him.'

'We'll be bothered all right,' I said. 'I know that man; and I know his landing point is somewhere around here and so do you, or what in hell are we all doing? Maybe you're just here for the fishing—but you haven't been manhandled by that big bastard.'

He turned angrily and the dark eyes burned in his head. The old flippant Larri had vanished, this was a new man, one totally unaccustomed to disobedience; but I too knew the uses of power. For a long moment we glared at each other, then he laughed gently, stepped forward and put an arm round each of us.

'Will you both do something for me—something very difficult?' he asked.

'Anything you like,' I said. 'What is it?'

'Nothing.'

I broke away and repeated incredulously, 'Nothing? Just let the sod get away with it?'

'No,' he said, 'I don't think he'll get away with it. I shall phone friend Lettcombe and he and Interpol can take it from here. I wanted to get him myself but you two have altered things. It's gone beyond the amateurs and I want you to promise to keep out of it.'

There was a long pause then Vashni said quietly, 'I promise, but I'm still going to find Chota Dal.'

He turned to me.

'Oh very well,' I said, 'I suppose you're right.'

Dawa came in silently and cleared the table. He looked as though he'd had a good night's sleep for once . . .

I was soaking out the vicissitudes of life with Kommer when Vashni wandered into the bathroom and joined me. I decided I would never quite get used to the wonder of that golden, hour-glass figure, and, paradoxically, the sense of rightness in being with her still produced a mild shock of surprise. In the drama of the last few days I had also forgotten how young she was; by the time I drove her out, the bathroom looked as though it had been used by a pair of hippos. I mopped up some of the water with my towel, and lay down on the bed to consider my next move. Sea light trickled through closed shutters patterning my thoughts. I woke suddenly from a curious dream; in it Vashni had come back, standing naked and inviting at the foot of the bed but the lovely outline melted and changed to the slight figure of her brother. His face as he stared at me was filled with compassion.

I dressed, slipped out of the house, and reached the harbour around noon. I found my kipper-faced friend pretending to mend nets at the end of the quay. He had struck me as having about as much community spirit as a conger-eel; whatever the solidarity of the village was hiding he would sell it. He broke when I put the third fiver on his net.

'All right,' he muttered, then shouted for the benefit of the blue-jerseyed loungers outside the pub. 'Waldo. Come here. Going out we are with this gentleman, for the fishing.'

The boat was old and patched and stank of ancient fish; but it pottered safely enough round to the western coast of Pen-Clawdd. I noticed that from the sea the house was invisible. Vashni was right, the cliff was a honeycomb, pockmarked with everything from great sea caves towering like cathedral naves, water moaning and sobbing through deep sunless galleries, to vast dry burrows that could have led to the earth's centre.

We wove through a graveyard of rocks, the two fishermen baiting lines and muttering in Welsh. Without too much sea running, and on a black night, the population of a small town could be packed away in that cliff. No one's mind was on the job but luck was against the fish and the bottom of the boat filled steadily with scaly bodies and cold reproachful eyes.

At last Kipper Face dropped a two-pound sea bass on the slithering heap and grunted, 'Reckon that's enough then eh?' Then he remembered the fivers and added, 'Sir.'

I looked at the face of the cliff and said casually, 'On a dark night there'd be more than fish to catch here.'

His eyes went blank.

'Oh come on, man,' I snarled impatiently. 'Where's the landing point? There's more Pakis come ashore here than fish.'

The other man spoke fiercely in Welsh, 'Pakis is it? And why not? At least they don't roost here fouling good Welsh land. Let them come as welcome guests and go to Birmingham and drink the stolen water from our drowned valleys as a gift from the Welsh.'

Kipper Face made soothing noises. 'Hush, man, hush. We've taken his money.'

His mate spat over the side. 'I'd as soon take his head. Why help a pompous bloody Englishman? We make good money from the black men—more money than he'll show us. Let them come I say; we are brothers in oppression.'

Kipper Face turned politely to me. 'My friend thinks we should go in now, sir.'

He opened the throttle and as the boat swung seaward, the ebb tide opened a wide wet mouth and showed a long, black, curiously shaped rock, almost under our prow. Kipper Face swore, wrenched the tiller over, and we slid past with a foot to spare. I looked back and the swell uncovered the rock again; stark against the red cliff, sculptured by some weird randomness of wave and tide into a twenty-foot-long coffin—perfect in every detail.

Kipper Face muttered apologetically, 'Yn fawr Craig. Forgotten the tide I had.'

I tried to keep my voice casual. 'What did you say it was called?'

'Yn fawr Craig, sir.' He was uneasy about his mate's outburst and very anxious to please. 'Dead Rock, sir— like a coffin it is see?'

'Yes,' I said slowly. 'I see.'

No one spoke again until we rubbed against the weed-scabbed stones of the quay. I climbed up first then gave Kipper Face a hand.

'*Diolch,*' he said automatically.

'*Peidiwch a son,*' I said. '*Prynhawn da.*'

'*Diawch!*' he whispered. I left them both staring after me and crossed the quay to the bar.

I had just demonstrated that, given a little encouragement the fish around Pen-Clawdd would crawl on to the quay and give themselves up, but the Ynysdeullyn fishermen thought differently; as on the last time I was here the bar was packed. I was beginning to get used to the reaction Traherne the Popular Visitor produced, and ordered a Scotch in a pre-sermon silence. Mari, the beautiful barmaid, upheld the hospitality of the pub by asking nervously how I was.

I said politely, *'Rwy'n dda iawn dialch.'* And Kipper Face from the open doorway, pointed out in a hoarse strained whisper that I was Welsh-speaking.

I had expected a reaction but not the one that came. They crowded round me in a swirl of tobacco smoke and beer and hours later I was dancing with the delectable Mari and buying enough ale to float all the disreputable fishing boats in the harbour. Later, I sat on the bar and explained that my father had been the best furnace man in the Valleys, that I was Welsh and proud of it, and then, craftily, what could they tell a countryman about the Indian landings?

They were careful; oblique but helpful. Yes, there were landings, a regular pattern of them. In fact if I cared to be on the north beach just before midnight I might see something interesting. Not their business mind, and do what I liked about it see? But the least they could do was help a Welshman—even one from the Valleys.

Ynysdeullyn was Prescelly Welsh; an overflow from the lovely hills behind the village. The Prescellys breed a secretive, proud people claiming the blood of King Arthur and live scattered in remote farms and hamlets through a hundred square miles of barren mountain. I was surprised and absurdly pleased that they had accepted me, but still puzzled they had told so much.

I assumed that Larri would, by now, have contacted Lettcombe. I have never allowed myself to be beaten to any goal, and before that cold professional mind took over I wanted to have the whole thing gift-wrapped and ready for him.

I spent the rest of the day dodging Vashni. She was damned nearly psychic where I was concerned and ten minutes alone with me would tell her I was planning something. It was a sultry day, the air hot, heavy as porridge in the lungs, the whole headland soaking up heat and tension like a solar battery. Over to the west, club-shaped clouds built slowly up the sky. I lay out on a gull-whitened ledge and watched the clear crystal of the sea flaw as the dark battlements built over it.

Through the stupor of the afternoon, thoughts tugged like puppies at the fringes of my mind. There was something I had missed. Far down the cliff a shapeless bundle opened lazy wings and spiralled up the thermal currents. Level with the ledge, savage golden eyes blazed into mine then the hawk was gone, towering up into the gathering storm. For a startled second I grabbed at an elusive answer, but the heat beat me down into sleep.

Dinner was not exactly festive. Vashni was perfectly aware that I had been avoiding her. Her usual idea of eating arrangements was to sit as near as possible without actually preventing my getting nourishment into the mouth. Tonight she was being the haughty princess at the far end of the ten-foot mahogany table. Larri sat at the other end and apart from his remarking that if any really urgent message needed to be passed he'd get a field telephone installed, the meal proceeded in dignified silence.

I got out of the house half an hour before midnight. The night was overcast and I kept to the path by the feel of gravel underfoot, using a torch only when I felt I might be taking the quick way down to the harbour. It was during one of these flashes that I caught a flicker of movement behind me. An old instinct, built in the tom-cat fights of Brynmawr back alleys, dropped me on all fours and rolled me sideways. Something pitched over me and hit the path with a solid thump; I twisted, flung myself forward and dropped heavily on it. From under me Vashni gasped breathlessly, 'I might have said you belong there but you choose the damnedest times to prove it.'

Larri hauled us to our feet. 'All right,' he said, 'suppose you stop being 007 and we join forces on whatever it is you're up to.'

The way to the north beach lay through the village and after hearing my story Larri insisted on calling out the policeman. He was the same man I had called before and he came reluctantly and suspiciously; it took my full name and title to shift him and he was still sure that Minister of State or not he was dealing with a deranged Englishman. As we climbed down into the cove, lightning sewed the low storm cloud into weird psychedelic patterns. There was not a breath of wind and, absolutely on cue, the sound of muttering voices and the splash of oars ran over the sea surface and multiplied in the rocks behind us.

I thought of what I had done to Kommer and realized, a little late, just how stupid we were being. What we needed just then was not three unarmed men and a girl but a nice solid torpedo boat to block the cove and half a regiment of Welsh Fusiliers on the cliff behind. The boats grounded and our idiot policeman stood up and gave tongue in the age old cry of the Law.

'Now then, now then; who's over by there? What's all this then?'

Things happened fast. Lightning glared and for a second I saw the beach like the underside of a lifted stone, swarming with life, then Vashni was gone from beside me and I took off after her, cursing my way towards the boats, dodging and crouching across the boulder-strewn beach. The lightning was continuous now. Dark-faced men tore wildly through the rocks but the movement patterned and drove me steadily towards the open sand at the water's edge. I saw Vashni, hair streaming in the storm-wakened wind, knee-deep in water, Larri and the policeman beside her. Our hunters thickened to a line and swept towards us howling an oddly familiar chant. Above the growing noise of the storm I heard Larri beside me, roar with sudden laughter, and had just time to wonder if he'd gone off his head when I recognized the tune: *Sospan Vach*, the ironic nonsense song of Wales— roared at every rugby international, sung bitterly on hunger marches, good-humouredly in their own pubs—an expression of the subtle contempt of Welsh for non-Welsh.

Then we were surrounded by a ring of dark grinning faces and a home-made banner was thrust into my face: 'THIS WAY TO BIRMINGHAM'.

Most of the village was there; a wave of jeering brown-stained faces surged about us, contorted with mocking laughter. The storm broke and, as the echoes of thunder died among the rocks, a voice called, 'Go back home, you half-bred English bastard.'

CHAPTER SIX

The purveyors of most religions go to a great deal of trouble denouncing pride; but if a man isn't a saint or a slave he must have something to give him guts enough to spit in God's eye.

I shouldered my way through the grinning mob and, when I reached the road, found Dawa sitting impassively behind the wheel of Larri's big Bentley. He scrambled out to open the door for me, but I swung past and turned east up the road to the mountains. I heard Vashni cry after me and walked on into the wind my stomach knotted in blind primitive rage. At that moment I could cheerfully have killed any or all of those damned villagers and fed their children to man-eating sharks. Larri with his usual insight didn't come after me—I imagine he must have tied his sister down, nothing else would have stopped her.

An hour later I was high on the mountain, moving blindly into a night black as a mole's backside. The whole situation sickened me. I was Traherne the Man of Destiny, and I should be moulding the fate of nations, not playing custard-pie comedy with a bunch of mountain Welsh. Then I stumbled, pitched full length on the invisible tarmac, and lay there cursing. I had only to step across the border into this damned country and my whole painfully built up pride in my achievements degenerated into farce.

I noticed I was thinking in Welsh and grinned; then remembered the look on the policeman's face when he saw the banner. Amusing that was; then, as the rain started, I sat on my bottom in the high dark of Carnenoc hill and howled with laughter.

There are two kinds of rain in Wales. One gentle and misty as a virgin's eyes, the other like the lower end of a waterfall. It's no land for compromise. From feeling the first tentative drops on the back of my neck, to being drenched and lost in roaring darkness took less than ten seconds; then I made the mistake of moving and found I had mislaid the road. There was nothing underfoot but invisible, boggy grass.

I spent what seemed like a very long time patting around on the bog with my hands and trying not to panic. I was in no danger. The night wasn't really cold and the worst that could happen was a long wait for daylight on the wet mountain; but there is something in wild high places where the earth has never been turned, that stirs shapeless, atavistic lumps from the dark porridge at the bottom of a man's brain. At last I could stand it no longer and trotted blindly forward into shrieking wet nothingness.

When I first saw the light I thought Larri must have driven up the road after me but it stayed motionless and I groped forward down a one-in-four slope falling to the waist in a miniature torrent on the way. I eventually beat on the door of a slate and stone cottage as though the black hound himself were taking the seat out of my trousers.

The door opened and a dark Silurian face peered out.

I remembered my manners and said politely, *'Noswaith dda.'*

'Bore da,' he said. 'Nearly morning now, see.'

'I don't give a damn if it's the bloody day of judgment. Can I come in out of this wet?'

He moved aside. 'No need for blasphemy now, man, is there?'

I stumbled over to a red hot range and a figure rose from a wheel-chair beside it.

The cottage was tiny: two rooms and a lean-to outback; the long, black range filled one wall of the living room/ kitchen, and a huge Welsh dresser, polished and hung with blue and white china reflected the glow of a Victorian oil lamp. There were four wooden chairs and a solid, scrubbed table. I don't suppose the room had changed in the last hundred years.

A woman's voice called querulously from the bedroom, but I was staring at the face of the figure beside me. The light had been bad when I last saw him, but someone who has tried hard to kill you is difficult to forget. It was my cliff-climbing Indian. He put his hands together and bowed. I looked him over and said, 'Someone's been feeding you. You want to watch it—it's easy to get hooked on eating.'

He bowed towards the Welshman who smiled sardonically. I jerked my thumb at the Indian.

'You realize he's illegal?'

The smile switched off abruptly. 'I don't give a monkey's fart,' he said. 'Whose laws—Westminster? English law? There's been one law for English and another for Welsh since the Prince died.'

'Owen Glyndwr Prince has been dead three hundred years,' the woman cried from the bedroom. 'The man's soaked. You let him in and he's your guest. Dry him and feed him and let's have a little less of the politics until you've done it.' The harsh voice died away.

We had been speaking Welsh and the Indian stared blankly at us. When I stripped he turned his head modestly away until I pulled on the rough trousers and jersey the Welshman tossed to me.

Anywhere else I would have been bogged down in a morass of explanations, but more than princely names came down over those years. The custom has died now of course, but when I was a boy, a stranger walking our street had the men knocking their caps and the women bobbing curtsies. Princely blood, princely manners, but it hasn't got them very far. No one goes hungry nowadays, but once over Offa's Dyke the affluent society is notably absent. The gigantic leech of England had lain across this country for half a thousand years draining it of wealth and men. I must say the wrongs of Wales had never kept me awake at night but at least I'd not expected gratitude like some of my fellow tradesmen in Westminster.

Hywel Jenkins, my host, farmed a hundred acres of stone outcrop and had found the Indian lying about on it the day after he left me. He took him in and fed him as matter of factly as he would a starved crag-bound sheep.

I took a long look at the dark figure opposite. Fed, washed, and without his knife, he was a good-looking man—about my own age and with a great deal more dignity. When I questioned him about the landings he folded his hands and shut his mouth tight.

At last I said, 'When I tell the police about you you'll go to prison.'

He shrugged almost imperceptibly and Jenkins said incredulously, 'Police? What sort of bloody Welshman are you?'

I pointed at him and said to the Indian, 'And he'll be inside with you. Do you want that?'

I jerked my head at the bedroom. 'Who's going to look after her then?'

Hywel said admiringly, 'What a bastard you are,' then to the Indian, 'Don't you mind him, Gupta boy. I can look after myself.'

Gupta looked from one to the other of us and twisted his fingers into knots.

'Why do you want to know this?' His voice was low, the English near perfect.

I said, 'You know why. This isn't just illegal entry; something's very wrong. Where's the rest of your family?'

It was guesswork but worth trying, and the effect was immediate. He put his head between his hands and wept.

'Leave the poor little sod alone,' Hywel shouted angrily.

I said, 'Shut up, I'm his best friend and he knows it.'

Gupta lifted his head and snarled something in his own language, then switched to English. The words poured out, thick and savage.

'I am a Brahmin and I have eaten filth. I was a landowner and I was herded like a pig. My family are dead. My wife and ...' his voice broke.

'Go on, Gupta,' I said harshly.

His brother was a perfectly legal immigrant in a good way of business in Wolverhampton, and had written to him to come over. His corner of India was in the grip of one of Providence's little jests—a five-year drought. If there'd been less than two million affected, and if India hadn't been bleeding herself dry just then dealing with the annual Bengal food crisis, his Government might have been able to do something for the province; but when people started dying of cholera he sold his land and moved the family to Delhi. They certainly didn't starve, but with two children, his wife, and her mother, Delhi wasn't cheap. As well as farming he'd been a craftsman in precious stones but the profession was overcrowded in the city. He was a good, hard-working, honest little man with getting on for ten thousand pounds in the bank so he tried very legally to come to England but of course found the quota had been filled by unskilled paupers. He just wasn't good at understanding English bureaucracy and kept on trying. Eventually someone put him in touch with the Organization.

He wasn't a fool. He turned half his capital into mixed uncut stones and used the rest as down payment for the conducted tour to Merrie England. He'd only have about twenty thousand pounds to pay off—on the usual terms of course—forty-five per cent interest. Provided they all went out to work and lived in one room they'd manage beautifully.

Being a Brahmin he was a considerable help and comfort to the paying customers on Kommer's pleasure cruise. On his trip no one got shot out of torpedo tubes and, of course, they had the advantage of not being depth-charged. Eighty of them came ashore very shaky but still cheerful and were led by Kommer's sailors into a great cave to wait for transport to their chosen towns. The place was lit by electricity and fitted out with comfortable bunks, cooking facilities, and lavatories. He reckoned they'd got it made, and when his wife had fed them they settled down for a good sleep.

When he woke he thought the place was a bit quiet, and then noticed that all but a dozen or so of the people had gone. One of the sailors told him the others were on their way to the Midlands and his turn would come soon. Everyone couldn't be transported at once. That seemed reasonable enough but there was something nagging the back of his mind, and it was several hours before he realized what it was. All the people who were left were solid citizens; he'd been with them now for several weeks and knew them well. No one had been stupid enough to admit it, but he was damned sure they were all, like himself, carrying a sizeable amount of portable wealth.

After breakfast the sailors took the rest of the paying customers, two at a time, through a very solid door set in the end wall of the cave. When they got round to Gupta's family he wanted them all to go together. The whole proceedings seemed sensible and orderly but he had a completely illogical feeling that something was wrong. One of Kommer's men explained in his fractured English that everyone had to be fitted out with used English clothes and given papers showing they had been in the country for at least three years; then they were taken to waiting transport. If more than two at a time emerged from the caves it might be noticed by the locals—again eminently reasonable.

Granny took the children off through the door and Gupta settled down, smoked a couple of cigarettes forbidden by his religion and caste, and eventually when he was called wandered off through the door holding his wife's hand. When the door shut they were in complete darkness. Gupta thought the lights had failed and called out cheerfully; then his wife's hand pulled away from him and he was alone.

Up to that point he had been a nice trusting little man. He'd been married ten years and it didn't seem a day too much. While he was telling me this bit I looked away; naked misery is very indecent. Often, when he was out on his farm or in the jewellery workshop, he used to slip back to the house just to make sure he wasn't fooling himself and he really did have a woman like that. Sometimes he wouldn't go back to work at all, and they'd dodge the servants and creep out to lie together in the forest like very young lovers.

When his wife was pulled away she made no sound and he found that horrifying. He put both hands to his face and screamed and something soft as a cat dropped round his neck. Then, for the first time in ten years he forgot his woman; he had other things to think of. A choking band of soft steel, a knee in his back, a hiss of indrawn breath in the darkness behind him.

He didn't die because the thing round his throat had trapped one of his hands beneath it. It seemed to him he took several lifetimes turning that hand and clawing for life against the numbing pressure. His spine was bent back like a full strung bow but he got one good rasping drag of air into his lungs and that gave him strength to reach back and grab behind him. He caught a wrist. A whip-cord tendoned wrist; but he was, by now, mad with fright, and madness can do the impossible. He turned that wrist as lightly as a well-oiled doorhandle and its owner called out and fell; then he ran forward into the darkness whooping and gasping for breath.

So far, talking had been a cathartic for him, purging a little of the essence of hell burning in his guts—but he didn't want to go on.

I said softly, 'Go on, Gupta,' and he stared unseeing past me and whimpered, 'My feet, my feet ...'

'What did you tread on, Gupta?'

Sweat rolled down his face.

'Bodies,' he whispered, 'I ran on bodies.'

He simply had no idea what happened to him after that. He seems to have run full speed through caves in pitch darkness, and of course, should have brained himself a dozen times. He came out a few feet above the sea on the north side of Pen-Clawdd. The village was half a mile away. He should have gone down and found my old friend the policeman, but he'd gone too far for normal behaviour. If anyone had a right to a psychiatrist's couch, he had; but I don't think he was completely mad, just atavistic. He had his knife, he knew his family were dead, and he was going to get their killers.

I had boarded Kommer's sub on its way back from Gupta's trip, and all the time I was in Hamburg, he had searched the headland for the reception cave. He crept down to the village at night and ransacked the dustbins and gardens for food. Don't forget he was a Brahmin. A practising, deeply religious Jew, eating raw pigs' feet in a gutter would have been ritualistically clean compared to what he was doing.

He never found the cave or any trace of it. He had no torch and there were a hundred or so ways into the cliff. On the evening I found him someone had started shooting at him. He didn't hear the gun so they would have been using a silencer, I suppose; he just felt little hurrying puffs of wind past his head, so they were very good and got very close. He'd thought I was one of them and came up after me. I remembered his knife and shuddered. If he'd been a little less starved he would have remodelled me extensively. When I left him that night he ran west into the mountains and Hywel's dogs found him the next morning.

He had one clue if you could call it that. In the struggle he'd pulled a ring from the hand he seized. He found it on his own finger the next day. I held out my hand; he tossed it over and Hywel got up and carried the lamp closer. It was a very massive ring and, I would have thought, very old. Not a signet, just a hoop of red gold half an inch wide, and, beautifully carved in bas-relief on the thick nugget of its top, a stooping hawk. I passed the ring back to Gupta and he slipped it on his finger.

'What are you going to do now?' I asked casually.

'I must kill the owner of this, Sahib.' His voice was eminently reasonable.

'What will you do afterwards?'

'Stay here,' he said, and looked towards Hywel.

The Welshman shrugged. 'He seems to be a farmer. I've a daughter away in Swansea with her auntie, but no son—and if I had one he wouldn't stay and farm this bloody quarry.'

Maybe I'd lost something by leaving Wales. It hadn't crossed Hywel's mind that this man in his home was an alien with a skin of tasteful chocolate-brown.

I turned back to Gupta. 'I'll help you but you must let the police have these men.'

He smiled unpleasantly but didn't speak. I thought of Vashni and realized I knew exactly how he felt. In the couple of hours I had known him I had become fond of the little man. I liked the courage of this dove angrily ruffling its feathers at a hawk; then I looked at the ring shining in the firelight, and shivered. Somehow I had to persuade him not to throw his life away; then I wondered why. What did one small, brown, ineffectual male human matter among nearly four billion? But then why had Vashni involved herself in the first place? If this one was a dove what was Chota Dal—a moulting sparrow dabbling in the gutter? The universe couldn't give a damn about such specks of planetary dirt; but Vashni had taught me the other side of the discomforting paradox. They were, at the same time, necessary as suns singing through space.

My clothes had dried out. I put them on and thanked Hywel for his hospitality. I kept my voice up but no sound came from the bedroom.

He grinned. *'Nes penelin nag arddwrn!'* Elbow and wrist are one—blood is thicker than water. Blood and water just about sums up Welsh history. Hywel nudged me. 'Wake up, boy; you taking him with you?'

'Yes,' I said. 'I need him.'

'Well keep him clear of the cops see; and send him back

123

in one piece. He knows how to milk the bloody cows.'

Hywel's farm had its own track, snaking down below the council road. The sun came up over the hill as we started and sucked up the night's rain until we walked under a gold-shot canopy of mist a foot above our heads. I was feeling good. With a little clever field work the whole racket could be rolled up. I would have loved to present the final parcel to Lettcombe, but I certainly wasn't going to tackle that deadly fox earth on my own. What I had to do now was get back to the house, contact Scotland Yard and get the local force briefed from there. My credibility rating with the Welsh constabulary was too low for more direct methods. Then I remembered Larri had said he'd already called London. With luck we might find Lettcombe waiting for us.

I tried to convince Gupta that he'd do more good as a witness than a one-man Light Brigade storming Kommer's H.Q., but when we reached the house he wouldn't come in. He connected the headland and everything on it with death—he wanted to stay in the open where he could see what was coming, and I didn't blame him. I left him on a small grassy mound outside the gates and went in to find Vashni; I knew he would trust her.

I got as far as the hall when she hurtled down the stairs and launched herself at me like a rugby international. Larri appeared from his office as I was trying to soothe her.

'Thank God you're back,' he said. 'All hell's broken loose.'

Vashni wailed, 'Darling, darling where have you been?' And the phone started ringing. I quietened Vashni by kissing her while Larri picked up the receiver.

He said, 'Yes. Yes, of course. Yes, he's back. Yes, I'll tell him. Yes, I have the telegram.'

'Couldn't we have a negative or two?' I said. 'So much affirmation makes me dizzy.'

With my arms full of Vashni I felt very good indeed.

He turned round and asked carefully, 'Tomas, you are quite sure of what happened on that submarine?'

I kissed Vashni again and came up for air. 'Well I may have got some of the detail wrong—it was a rough trip. Why?'

He turned away, then back. 'That was the Home Office. They want you up in London at once.'

'Damn them,' I said angrily. 'They're not my department.'

'The Prime Minister wants you,' he said quietly, 'and, I gather, the Admiralty. I gave Lettcombe your story and ...' There was an embarrassed pause. 'They think the whole thing is ... fantasy.'

Vashni twisted indignantly in my arms. 'But I was there,' she said. 'I can confirm it all.'

He stared at us silently then handed me a telegraph form.

TRAHERNE. PEN-CLAWDD HOUSE. YNYSDEULLYN. PEMBROKE. NAVY DENY PICKING UP DEAD INDIAN NATIONAL. CIVILIAN SUB.U847 REGISTERED HAMBURG EXAMINED ON HIGH SEAS FOUND COMPLETELY IN ORDER ON LAWFUL OCCASIONS. COMPLAINTS LODGED BY CAPTAIN WITH BRITISH AND GERMAN AUTHORITIES OF DEPTH CHARGE ATTACK. REPORT FROM C.I. LETTCOMBE SUGGEST YOU RESPONSIBLE INFORMATION ON WHICH NAVY ACTION REQUESTED. MATTER EXTREMELY

The message originated from the P.M.'s office.

I had been a politician too long not to know my priorities. I looked up from the form and snapped, 'The media?'

'I don't know how it was done but Lettcombe says there's a D-notice on it.'

Well that was O.K. for a while. Obviously I still had some friends and a career—just. The only muzzle you can get on a press hound is a D-notice—'publicity not in the interest of national security'—and like all good dogs they paw it off as soon as possible.

Vashni wailed, 'It *is* true. It *is* true.'

I thought of those torpedo tubes and shuddered. Well, I'd beaten more slippery ones than this but I couldn't have my chief ally sending for the little men in white coats to take me away.

'Larri,' I said gently, 'Vashni *was* with me you know.'

He moved aimlessly across to the front-door and stared out on to the sun-lit hill. The mist had lifted, the sea winked cheerfully far below, and distant morning noises rose from Ynysdeullyn. He answered me without turning his head.

'My sister is in love with you, Minister.'

Well, he hadn't the monopoly of formality. 'I believe I have that honour,' I said stiffly.

He spun round. 'Oh don't be such a bloody fool! I'm glad she is, but she's—not an Englishwoman.'

'I noticed that.'

'You don't understand do you? Indian women do what their men want.' There was a long silence. 'And say what they know their men wish them to say.'

'The hell with that,' I said. 'I'll bring you someone you *will* believe.'

I ran out the open door and down the drive, but I needn't have hurried. Gupta had followed instructions and stayed put. It hadn't been difficult for him. He lay on his back. His eyeballs were on his cheeks, blood trickled from the empty sockets and the twisted mouth. A dull red welt circled his throat. I touched the dark hair and the head fell limply sideways; his neck had been neatly broken at the fourth vertebra.

An Olympic runner might just have beaten me back to the house but I doubt it. I skidded to a stop in the hall, heard Larri's voice in his office, and dived for his door. It opened as I reached it and we ended in a heap on the floor. Vashni shrieked, then I was out of the house towing Larri behind me. The whole performance could not have taken more than five minutes.

When we reached the mound, Gupta had gone. I did all the right things in the right order. I searched the area; not difficult, the house was the only cover for half a mile, so I searched that and found only a gaping Dawa cleaning saucepans in his kitchen. I believe in magic about as much as I do in a career politician's conscience, but the back of my neck tingled when I stood again on the mound. A strong man could have run fifty yards with the body and thrown it over the cliff edge. I'd already spent several vertiginous minutes peering at the white-capped water two hundred feet below and it was very possible

Gupta was down there; but unless he was prepared to go with his victim where was our strong man?

It hardly seemed worth it—with this one I hadn't even Vashni to back me up, but I filled Larri in on events and waited for the reaction. I waited a long time. He fell back on the inscrutability of the east, showing about as much expression as a bronze Buddha. I stood several minutes of this then said irritably, 'I'm going to get that policeman and a boat and search the sea at the foot of the cliff. If necessary I'll have the whole damn village out searching.'

'They'd just think you were getting even for last night,' Larri said wearily. 'Don't you realize no one will believe this man exists?'

I said, 'No one, Larri?' and he had the grace to look ashamed; then he cheered up. 'What about this farmer who sheltered him?' He asked excitedly. It was the obvious solution. I ran in to telephone then had a vivid mental picture of the Law asking Hywel Jenkins if he had sheltered an illegal immigrant.

I could smell sandalwood and knew Vashni was standing somewhere behind me. I spoke savagely without turning. 'All right, phone the nearest bin and tell them I'm seeing little green men and invisible Brahmins.'

She made a small noise in her throat like an unhappy child and the scent faded.

Larri came softly up and put a hand on my shoulder. 'You were supposed to be going on holiday, Tomas,' he said gently. 'Remember? Go and catch a plane and lie in the sun—and take Vashni with you. You've been exhausted ever since we met you and you need a rest.'

'Don't worry,' I said, 'I'm going. I must thank your Highness for your hospitality, please give my best regards to your sister.'

I was throwing clothes into a suitcase when I became aware again of her scent. She was standing in the doorway her hands twisted anxiously together. I went on with the packing and she said, 'Oh darling,' very quietly. I left the case and went over to the bathroom. She was wearing a sari and I wanted her so much I felt sick.

'Darling,' she said again. 'Please, darling.'

'You believe me about Gupta of course,' I said.

'Yes.'

'Quite sure?'

'Oh yes, darling.'

'The faithful Indian wife agreeing with her man?'

'There's worse ways to be than that.' Her voice was so low I could barely hear the words.

I said, 'Speak up, woman,' and she said loudly, 'Do you have a better recipe than that for living together?'

'Who's talking about living together?' I said brutally. 'I just want truth; I'm in a trade where it's in short supply. I never wanted a permanent woman, but if I did have one I'd want complete honesty—see?'

'Yes, darling.'

She had dropped her voice again, and I raised mine. 'I deal in subterfuge, double talk, half truths. I could make you a two-hour speech on any damn subject you like to name and it wouldn't have a single hard fact in it—and you'd think it was wonderful. Do you want that as a basis for living together?'

'No, darling.'

'All right then, but I've seen it happen. Good, reasonable, honest men and women; ordinary run-of-the-mill people treating each other civilly and considerately. Then they go and live together or get married and start behaving with about as much mutual trust as secret agents. Good God, I've known couples married a year who wouldn't tell each other the right time. Do you want to live like that?'

I could just hear the whisper. 'No, darling.'

'For Christ's sake stop being so submissive,' I shouted. 'I tell you this wouldn't work. How can I do my job anyway with a woman round my neck? I'm Tomas Traherne, the bloody saviour of this bloody country; when I want something I get it—and I don't want you.'

She looked strangely at me; the eyes huge, piercing and dark. The beautiful face calm, remote as the hidden water mirror in a well. I dragged my eyes from her. 'I've done well in this business, haven't I? Go on—agree with me!' I found I was shouting again and made a savage effort to control my voice; then I ticked off the points on my fingers. 'I decide to help you find a poor little Indian bastard; so all right, you can stop worrying—Traherne has it in hand—and an ordinary decent man driving a car for me gets squashed. Then I really start to help and someone gets used as a torpedo by a fugitive from a comic war film; and now, real amusing this one, my little Brahmin mate gets his head nearly sawn off—only that one doesn't count does it because he's a figment of my imagination? You want protection, just call in Traherne.'

I threw the suitcase on the floor, dropped heavily on

the bed, and turned my head away from her. 'What in hell do you want from me anyway?' I whispered.

In one movement she slipped the sari from her shoulders and knelt naked across me on the bed.

'This, Lord,' she said.

The firm breasts sank down and the wide wet mouth closed on mine.

No one came near us all through that long, hot day. At one point she padded off into the still recesses of the house and brought back burgundy, brown bread and cheese. We ate, made love, and slept. All thought faded. My mind became a still pool reflecting only the treasure house of her moving body.

Later, I lay looking through the wide window into a darkening, purple sky. I was at peace and knew exactly what I must do. I had pitted myself against tough, unscrupulous villains on their own ground and using their own weapons. Now I would get back into my framework that I should never have left. Vashni lay sprawled across me drowned in sleep and joy of fulfilment. I stroked the damp, passion-tangled strands of hair. She was as much part of me as my own limbs; it was unthinkable that danger should come near her. As I moved she laughed in her sleep and turned on to her back. I slipped off the bed and started to dress.

I was going straight to London and she was coming with me. This whole mess was falling into its right perspective. I smiled to myself; in a year's time I could have the destiny of fifty million people in my hands and all the power I had ever desired. I must have been mad to involve myself personally in a stupid, sordid and dangerous enterprise of this kind. I was dealing with a cold, clever and devious brain running a murderous criminal organization for very high rewards, and I didn't think Kommer's pink skull housed it. Someone who could discredit me with Larri and my own party chief was not the animal with whom I had spent that Hamburg night. I went into the bathroom and started shaving. Whoever he was I'd teach him that tiger riding had very definite disadvantages.

My mind moved like a machine. Ten minutes with the P.M. would straighten out Lettcombe and the Admiralty. My chief wanted out. He was coming up for sixty, a cynical, embittered, sick man, but he wanted to get out on his own terms and I was the only one he could trust to guarantee him that. It was still Recession so I couldn't start a whispering campaign in the House; but I could threaten to call in the press and give an interview that would open up a few of my alleged friends like sardine cans. For years I'd fostered a legend of my vast secret files—I'd get what I wanted all right. If I told them to parade Whitehall sucking ice lollies they'd do it.

In twelve hours I'd control enough security forces to seal off this whole stretch of country, and they could sit quietly down and wait for Kommer and the big boy to show. Interpol could handle the Continent and India and if Lettcombe started shoving Larri around, I'd drop the word among the higher police echelons that it could turn out to be a bad year for knighthoods. With the professionals handling it Vashni and I could get on with some living. It was time I woke her.

I put on the bedside lamp and kissed her eyes, her

mouth, and the soft insides of her spread thighs. She made small contented noises and put out a hand to stroke my hair ...

Someone started screaming inside my head.

The perfection of her body was flawed. A flaw almost hidden by the softness of pubic silk. A design no more than an inch square, a tattoo—old and faded but filling my whole field of vision. The outline was of a stooping hawk.

CHAPTER SEVEN

Logically, I should have stayed put and used the discovery as a trump card, but I was beyond logic. My flesh crawled. This woman was irrevocably mine. I had never before given myself, never relaxed my guard. I had lived thankfully without human affection; even in sex there had been always a certain revulsion—an impatience that my body should need this labile wallowing. With Vashni, whatever she was, whoever she was, the thing was done. Being unable to live without another person is a trite and sickening fantasy; I had believed that and was now very properly rewarded. I was not even sure when it had happened, but the woman sprawled on the bed was myself and I her. We were fused as a weld fuses steel; the join far stronger than the basic stuff.

I backed away from her, my hands to my mouth. It was lucky I had dressed or I would have run naked out into the dusk; I didn't realize I had left the house until I was through the gates, then I stopped and looked back. I could see leaf-dappled light from the room where she still lay. I tried to force my mind to logical thought. She carried the mark of the killer but there could be, there *must* be an explanation; the only one that occurred to me nearly burned out my brain.

I turned slowly and looked seaward. The last purple light of day flared up on the rim of the world and silhouetted the mound on which Gupta had died. I didn't want to think about Gupta or the way he looked when

I last saw him. As I stared he edged craftily into my mind the picture horribly overlaid by Vashni's passion distorted face. The next thing I knew I was standing sweating and panting outside the village bar, and from inside was coming a great deal more noise than usual.

One thing Traherne could be relied on to do in those parts was stop a party in its tracks; the silence when I shoved open the door was of good vintage quality. If there'd been a corpse behind the bar it couldn't have been given more respect. I shouldered my way through the silent men and told Mari to give me whisky. Modern scientific aids to drinking hadn't reached Ynysdeullyn, and she started pouring into a small pewter measure. I leaned over, took the bottle from her, and drank straight from it. No one commented; perhaps they'd seen it done on television. The landlord waddled angrily forward; I stared at him over the bottle and he found he had business in his cellar. I think he saw something in my face that disagreed with him.

The Scotch got straight down to the job. The disturbing pastiche of Vashni and the dead Gupta wavered and separated, and I found I had developed a good sound ambition to finish that bottle and get on to the next. When, if ever, I left that bar they were going to pour me over the threshold. I became aware of something tugging at my arm and a voice muttering indignantly, 'Wrong that is, drinking like that.' Some bright spark had thought of using the law to get rid of me. I tossed a wad of notes to Mari and patted the policeman on the shoulder.

'Paid for,' I said. 'Have one yourself, my fine watch dog.'

'You should be getting from here,' he said. 'You are not wanted here.'

I was tired of this policeman. I put my bottle down carefully, twisted one hand into his tunic and one in his crotch and rushed him backwards through the doorway. Out on the quay I swung him up and heaved; when the splash came I went back inside. They had been having a *cymanfa*—an impromptu concert. There was a small platform of barrels with planks laid over, built for the singers at one end of the long room. I walked towards it weaving slightly and the crowd opened up and let me through. No one dropped any pins but the classic conditions were there to hear one.

Getting up on the platform took some time but I made it, then I carefully examined the remains of my Scotch— the first part of my ambition was in sight. I made sure of it and tossed the empty bottle into the crowd. Someone caught it and I said pleasantly in Welsh, 'What are you celebrating my fine murdering Silurian dogs? Another delivery of prime corpses under Pen-Clawdd?'

One of them shouted, 'Don't call us names, you half-bred bastard!'

My skull seemed to swell until it moulded into the corners of the room, then collapsed on itself squeezing my brains like an orange. Twenty years of conditioning fell away.

I said thickly, 'I am Welsh, you gutter-dropped son of a bitch. Come over by here and I'll prove it.'

No question now of throwing me out; when it comes to a fight, the Irish are convent-bred nuns to the Welsh. They made a ring and I dropped lightly into it. He was a very big man topping me by a couple of inches, arms hanging like an ape's from gigantic shoulders and ending in hands the size of dinner plates, but an incipient beer paunch swelled out his ragged fisherman's jersey. From a corner Kipper Face said surprisingly, 'Shake hands they should and fight to rules.' Perhaps he remembered my fivers.

'Of course,' I said, and held out my right hand. As the man took it I sank a left into his beer belly. He made an explosive noise like a startled cow and fell towards me. I smashed a right hook into his toppling face and stepped aside as he went down. The floorboards shuddered and Kipper Face sighed, 'Neat, but very dirty, mind.'

Brynmawr had come back. Before I was fourteen I had a reputation as a fighter that brought every young bull in the valley out against me. Some nights I fought until my bruised fingers refused to function and I was fed victory beer by sycophantic hands. I can't remember ever being beaten.

I took two more of them singly before they lost their temper and came at me in a pack. Then I reverted joyfully and completely, using chairs, feet and teeth.

I had a handful of someone's crotch and a mouthful of foul-tasting fisherman's ear when the noise died and the bodies were hauled off. Mari stood over me, a five-foot fury with a wooden mallet in her hand. The men backed from her and I pulled myself shakily up on to the remnants of the platform.

'Anyone else like to dispute my nationality then?'

'*Jawch* no!' My first victim said. 'You fight Welsh;

'folded my guts up like an old sheet you have.'

I said, 'Right then. Who's buying the beer here tonight —Captain bloody Kommer? Tired are you of being lap dogs for the English but you bring in Germans to pay you for murder?'

'Man, man,' Kipper Face said soothingly, 'no one is murdered now. Very profitable it is, we just look the other way sometimes, see? And Trevor the Taxis and his sons take a few blacks for a drive.' He looked slyly at me. 'To Birmingham maybe?'

That fetched a laugh. The composite face of Vashni and Gupta swam horribly back into my brain.

'Do you know what is going on?' I whispered. 'You think it amusing, do you? Funny is it to sit here fooling the English and filling their towns with immigrants? Would you like to know how they live when they get there? Ten in a room and fifty to a smashed lavatory. Different to you, are they? Don't need human conditions, is it?'

I had them now; they knew about exploitation.

One of them said heavily, 'Aye you may be right, but we didn't ask them to come—and that's not murder.'

I'd been in better speech-making condition but I put it over carefully and in detail. I told them about Gupta and how he died, then topped it up with a description of the torpedo room and what Gupta had run over in the caves. They tried hard not to believe; admitting to murder, even by proxy, is not easy. Then through the mutterings and whispers a voice said, 'Dead is he, boy?'

Hywel Jenkins stood just inside the door.

'Yes.'

I watched him closely. A short, thickset man, fifty perhaps but only the eyes showed it. He crossed to the bar.

'Give me a drink, Mari.'

The girl poured him half a glass of rum. He drank it carefully, not sipping but with a smooth, practised motion, then peered through the smoke and took in the broken chairs and battered customers.

'Trouble then with the fishmongers, *bach*?'

'No,' I said. 'We were discussing the Welsh language.'

He swung round and spat on the floor at their feet. It was not something I would have liked to do. There were a lot of them. While we had fought I had known it was mostly play. No one was supposed to get really hurt, but this was direct insult. I waited for the explosion and they shuffled their feet and looked sheepishly at each other.

'Gupta was a nice boy,' Hywel said quietly. 'Gwennie liked him—won't be anyone to help with the cows now either.'

For a big man I move fast, but I would have turned in a performance like a ruptured snail beside Hywel. As he finished speaking he had the nearest man down on his knees. One hand gripped his throat, the fist of the other rested on the bridge of the nose, first and fourth fingers jammed horribly into the eye sockets.

'Do you want to see again, *bach*?' he whispered. The man made an animal noise deep in his throat.

'Ah.' Hywel gave a gentle sigh. 'Then tell me who killed my friend.' The man sobbed and pawed at Jenkins's coat. No one moved to help him.

139

'Leave him alone,' I said. 'They all did it by working for Kommer; Gupta's not alone; there's a butcher's shop under Pen-Clawdd.'

He sighed again and turned back to the bar. Mari filled his glass. The man shuffled to the door still on his knees, clawed it open and went out.

I signalled to Mari. After that I needed a drink, but out of deference to the natives I used a glass this time. All my life I'd had to make up my mind fast about men. When I first met Hywel I knew he was something special, but I'd not had time then to pursue it. He was watching me now with a curious expression on his face. I spoke in English, 'All right, who are you?'

'Best forget it, boy,' he said. 'I know who you are. Just remember you're Welsh when you get to be head of the school, eh?' I didn't answer and he said, 'There's more to politics than Plaid Cymru in this land of our fathers, Tomas.'

We were still speaking English. 'What were you in the Hitler war, Hywel?'

'Bright aren't you?' He laughed shortly. 'Resistance.'

'And you kept up the old trade. What do you resist now?'

He gave me a hard look. 'Settle the Welsh problem when you are in power will you, Tomas?'

I looked down at my empty glass and said blandly, 'What Welsh problem?'

He laughed and the first man I had beaten came up and said, 'Mr Jenkins you knew about the smuggling; we didn't deceive you.'

'And the killings.'

'So help us, Hywel,' another man said, 'we didn't know. We've always thought they all went up country.'

'So they did,' I said. 'As long as they had only a few bob on them—there's a double profit from the rich ones.'

'Do you know who's running it?' Hywel asked.

The Scotch heaved back into my throat. I swallowed and made myself speak carelessly. 'Kommer, I suppose.'

'Ah no, Tomas; he's a mad bull. This is fox work—one of my own kind.' He peered sideways at me. 'Going up to London now, is it—call in the big battalions?'

A lifetime ago that was exactly what I had planned. Hywel was a fox all right.

I frowned and said seriously, 'Surely the first thing to do is to get into those caves. These men must know how, and you seem to have influence.'

Kipper Face answered; like all jackals he liked to keep near the source of supply. 'Get in all right.'

Hywel raised one eyebrow, 'Yes, Ifor?'

It was strange to hear him given a name when I'd thought of him as Kipper Face for so long.

'Finding one cave would be the trouble, see. The old name was Bryn Morgrug—proper ant hill too, it is. Thousands of passages and caves.'

'How do you know when a landing is coming?' I asked.

He hesitated and waited until Hywel nodded. 'The captain sends word and we keep away. Then we ferry them off Craig y Meirw at low tide and pass them to Trevor's boys.'

I nodded. 'How many to a shipment?'

He shrugged. 'Varies. Fifty; never more than sixty.'

The torpedo room held eighty. If Kommer had been going for only five years ... I made a rapid calculation of the discrepancy, and felt sick. Hywel broke into that very unpleasant line of thought.

'London still, is it?'

'It should be.' My voice was sour, then I said quickly, 'Kommer has a lot of fire power. Can you tell me why we shouldn't call in the proper authorities?'

Hywel had said he was a fox and I believed him. At all costs I must head him off a scent that might lead to ... my mind wouldn't complete that thought, but at least I had a shrewd idea now of who Jenkins was.

Wales has always fought bitterly and hopelessly for its existence as a nation. Since the death of the great Prince it has been more or less an occupied land. Most English people, and a surprising number of Welsh, would dismiss this as nonsense, regarding the Principality in the same light as any other strongly regional area in the island, but it's true enough. Somehow racial integrity has survived. Perhaps the nineteenth-century rape of the country's natural wealth actually helped to preserve the nation—misery and oppression often mould and bind a people more than prosperity. Eventually the country submitted, and its lifeline to the past—the native culture embodied in the language—was slowly frayed by contempt and neglect. The land emptied; successive governments passed motions deploring economic stagnation in Wales; and the Welsh Office turned over in its sleep.

Now a generation had come that had had enough. God knows what caused it. Perhaps the undertow of the waves of war pulled them out to a depth where they could either save themselves as a nation, or drown for ever. Revival of the language was the foundation stone of a new native culture. It expressed itself in dozens of small movements—mostly talk and eisteddfods, but under it all a militant presence was making itself felt. Small campaigns, defacing signposts in English, refusal to acknowledge courts not conducted in Welsh, straws, but lately the straws were pointing in one direction. Someone with training to work out the logistics of guerilla war had taken a hand. Hywel?

He broke in on my thoughts. 'I'll take Kommer. It could have been done years ago but we ...'

He regarded me steadily. A shrewd commander assessing a possible renegade.

'Keep it Welsh, Tomas. It's our job; we encouraged him. I've been busy elsewhere but I've had about as much sense as a high school girl. Squalling about Cymru while he used us all to cover murder.' His mouth tightened. 'But we know now and we'll deal with it.'

A good man Hywel—keep him thinking about Kommer at all costs.

I spoke hurriedly, 'How do we know when he's coming ashore?'

'Watcyn Jones Wireless is a clever young man, especially with the short waves; picks up the ships talking; hobby of his, see?'

I put my hand in my pocket to pay for another drink; among the handful of change was a scrap of paper. I put the coins on the counter and unfolded it carefully. I knew the illiterate, childish hand at once; it was identical with the few scrawled words of the note I had found after being attacked beside the river, but my unknown correspondent was getting more ambitious. This time there was a whole page. I read it once and pushed it along the bar to Hywel. He read aloud slowly, for some reason translating into English.

'I still may not tell you who I am. I dare not for my life. Please I want no reward—just that you will not try to find me. I told an Indian man about Pen-Clawdd caves, he gave me money. He told me Indians would be smuggled from there but I swear I did not know about the killings. I was at the meeting in London because I went up with some of the smuggled men. I was ashamed when you spoke and I gave you that message but I did not know there was murder. Please do not try to find me. I am in great fear. Soon I shall know who it was I first told. He had a stocking on his face, but when he gave me money I saw a great ring with a bird on it. He was a small man. Soon I will know then I will tell you because of the murders ...'

Hywel pursed his lips and whistled tunelessly.

I said, 'Well, that narrows it. You'll gather I had another of these earlier. This makes him local.'

'Does it?'

'Damn it! Of course it does, man,' I said impatiently. 'It was put in my pocket tonight. You know them all here and you'll be able to find him.'

He picked up the note between finger and thumb. 'How long has this been in your pocket, Tomas?'

'A few minutes, obviously.'

'Sure?'

He was examining the paper carefully. My heart turned

over. This was a fox who could lay traps. I said nothing.

'Very grand the Welsh language,' he murmured. 'Very musical.' He raised his voice, 'Ifor?' Kipper Face shuffled eagerly forward. 'Have a drink, Ifor.'

He folded the note leaving only the blank space at the bottom showing then spoke in English. 'Write for me, Ifor—in Welsh. Write, "I saw a great ring with a bird on it"—lyrical that is, Ifor.'

The man looked doubtful but took the proffered pen and scrawled laboriously. After a while Hywel took the paper from him. 'Take your drink away, Ifor.' His voice was still gentle. He spread the note out again.

'Observe.'

Kipper Face had never been the pride of his teachers. His writing beat even my informant for sheer illiteracy of form but the words were clear, and they were not the words of the note. This was spoken Welsh—the patois of the countryside. The note, illiterate as it looked, was in classic Welsh—the language as it would be taught to a foreigner. I should have seen it myself but I had been an Englishman for too long.

Hywel pointed a stubby finger. 'Observe the lovely use of the circumflex, now even I would not do that. But then I have never studied Welsh, *bach*.'

The longer I stayed with him the more dangerous he would be. There could be no question now of bringing in security forces and Lettcombe; they would do too good a job.

I said, 'If you think you can take Kommer, I'm with you.' I picked up the note. 'I'll let you know when I hear from this character again. You tell me when your radio ham gets the next message. I can bring only two men. Larishnapur and his servant.'

'Don't worry,' he said, 'I can bring fifty.'

'Kommer has guns.'

He laughed. 'Has he now? You go back to Pen-Clawdd and let me worry about guns.'

Every step back to the house was like wading through treacle. There was a part of my mind that insisted, logically and correctly, that if I spent more than a few hours away from Vashni in future, it would not be responsible for its actions. The part I was using for immediate purposes was producing the treacle effect. It didn't want me to take it within a thousand miles of her. What it wanted was to get on a nice fast vehicle and go somewhere useful, like say, Tokyo. Its arguments were limited —just Gupta's dead face and the statistics supplied by Ifor—but it used them effectively.

By the time I arrived at the house, I had developed a good enough case of incipient schizophrenia to provide any competent psychiatrist with years of work. I used the back-door. Come to think of it, the back regions are a natural venue for politicians. At a good many general gatherings of the electorate over which I have presided, the audience has been either too enthusiastic, or too vengeful for me to risk the normal way into a building; but I welcomed Pen-Clawdd's tradesman's entrance for other reasons.

Somewhere upstairs Vashni would be waiting. She would be wondering why I had left her, and she would want me back. I stood in the darkness of the kitchen, my eyes screwed shut against a greater darkness. In that moment I knew, whatever she was, whatever monstrous pit of evil had spawned her perfection, I could never leave her. Through the silence of the house I became aware of a strange mewing sound; I opened my eyes, realized it was my own voice and put out a hand to steady myself. The almost red hot top of an ancient cooking range was beside me, and the immediacy of pain shocked me back to reality.

I found Larri still in his office. In spite of a conviction that several lifetimes had elapsed since I left the house, the Congreve clock on the mantelshelf showed an hour before midnight. He put down his pen and looked up warily.

I said, 'I've just been down to the village.'

He nodded and I threw the note down on the desk.

'I seem to have acquired this from one of your neighbours.'

He picked the paper up and studied it doubtfully. His reaction surprised me; I had expected further disbelief, anger—anything but what I got.

He tossed me a pencil.

'Write me something, Tomas.'

'What?'

'Anything.'

I pulled a pad towards me and scribbled, 'Now is the time for all good men and true ...'

I had forgotten he had kept the original message. It was on the desk and he arranged the notes with my scrawled sentence between them; as he studied the three pieces of paper I turned my head away and looked at the beautiful clock. After a long five minutes the rolling ball in its base tilted the escapement balance noisily, and Larri sighed.

'I am terribly sorry, Tomas. I thought you ... you see these notes ...' He tried again. 'I thought perhaps the strain ...'

'You thought I was nuts.'

He looked at me and grinned. 'Frankly yes.'

'Why the change of mind?'

He pressed a concealed spring and a small panel swung open in the desk. 'I wanted to talk to you. You weren't with Vashni and you weren't in your room, but this was.' He smoothed out a sheet of crumpled paper. 'I found it on your pillow. I thought it just possible you'd written it yourself.'

I took it from him. 'My correspondent seems a really conscientious lad,' I said drily.

The spiky, illiterate scrawl was in the same immaculate Welsh. I translated as I read:

'You found the dead rock and I am now in danger and must go away. There are people who will kill me because I told you. I think I have found the man who was missing. The sweeper man you talked about at the meeting. I cannot write it all so I must talk to you. This man had been dead for a long time when I found him. I will show him to you and tell you other things then I must go away. Meet me tonight at Bedd Morris beside the stone. Come at midnight. *You must come alone.*'

I put the paper down and Larri swept it with the others into his secret drawer. He glanced at the clock. 'Come on,' he said urgently, 'we've got under an hour.'

I caught him up in the hall. 'Where's this Bedd Morris?'

'Five miles into the mountains; there's a standing stone, a damned great thing—Neolithic, I suppose—you can see it from the road but it's a devil of a scramble to get to it up the hill; we've got to move.'

The phone rang. Dawa glided in, picked it up, listened for a moment and handed it to me. Ifor's voice whispered in Welsh against a background of static.

'Mr Traherne?'

'Yes?'

'The message has come—it is tonight.'

'Where are you?'

'At the inn.'

'Where is Hywel?'

'At his farm, I am going there in a few minutes.'

I thought quickly. 'How much time have we?'

'Full tide in two hours, they will land then.'

The line went dead. Larri had sent Dawa scuttling out, and I heard the great Bentley purring up to the front-door. My mind took the data, examined it, and delivered answers.

I had to keep this appointment alone or my bird would fly. It could be a trap, but all the more reason to be alone. In any case I needed someone to take a message to the Jenkinses' farm. At all costs Larri must not innocently give this information to his sister; the first job, therefore, was to get him away from the house. After that we would smash Kommer and through him the rest of the organization. I could think about Vashni afterwards, but the job must now be done without official help.

I raced out towards the Bentley shouting, 'I want another car; don't argue, just tell Dawa to get it.'

Larri stared but gave the order.

'Do you know a farm called Carnenoc?' I asked.

'Jenkins. Yes, he's well known. Carnenoc's on the west road—Bedd Morris on the east, they both cross the mountain.'

'Good. I want you to go there. Tell him what's happened, and say I'll join you in two hours at the most. If I *don't* come, go with Jenkins anyway and do what he tells you. He knows what he's at and he's going to smash Kommer.'

He gave me a long look then said, 'Right, Tomas. Take care.'

Dawa put the Bentley in gear and it whispered out through the gates. I climbed into the other car—a ponderous vintage Lancia. The glove pocket was open and inside I found a small efficient-looking automatic; it seemed that Larri had played rough games before and wanted me to have the right equipment. I switched on, set the advance/retard and pressed the starter. The Bentley moved like an elegant shadow. This tank had been built in an age that equated speed with noise; the exhaust echoed against the house like thunder, but above it I heard my name.

Vashni stood on the broad balcony and, as the car moved she held out her arms towards me; the sari, draped hastily over her naked body, streaming away from her in the rising wind.

CHAPTER EIGHT

I have never subscribed to the opinion that when a car is really outdated it becomes automatically a covetable article. Vehicles are for efficient progress from A to B. However, once you got used to its noise, the Lancia was superb; it ate up the five miles of convoluted mountain road in ten minutes. That may not qualify for a book of records but Prescelly roads were built strictly for sheep.

As it was I wasted another five minutes by overshooting. Larri had told me to use a ruined cottage as a marker, and I was touching seventy when I passed it. I backed up laboriously, eased the Lancia into a soggy cattle yard, and started up a dubious track that originated at a field gate. The only mark I had was a curving line of lesser darkness where mountain and sky met a few hundred feet above, and a vague hint of a towering mass occluding the background stars. I had a torch but was not going to make a target of myself until I knew exactly what was waiting up there.

After a while it became very much easier to keep to the track. I didn't discover why until I sank gratefully down on the summit ridge and saw the lights of a car sweeping up from the valley. In the reflected glow I could pick out the bulk of the standing stone a few yards to my left. The car could contain a late homing farmer, but if so he'd been drowning the woes of agriculture in drink. The beams swung dizzily as he screamed through hairpin bends and I found myself hoping he'd get well past before the inevitable crash—I was too busy to give first aid. The cottage lit up like a battered piece of *son et lumière*; there was a squeal of brakes, I caught a glimpse of the Lancia crouching in its mud patch, then the night became very dark indeed.

I pressed myself into the stone rubble of the mountain and waited. Someone was coming up after me. He either didn't possess a torch, or had the same cogent reason as myself for not using one. He was moving much too quietly to be heard above the keening of the wind, but a sound primitive instinct told me someone was there— the nape of my neck prickled like an angry dog.

After a while I remembered Larri's gun and got it out. Strangely enough, until I had to use Kommer's piece of portable artillery, I had never handled a firearm. I'd had many invitations to shoots but the reduction of tame, coloured chickens to small bloody messes had never struck me as an amusing sport. Now I wished I hadn't been so superior. A little tuition, even with a sporting gun, might have showed me how to check if this particular equalizer was loaded and just where its safety catch was situated. I lay still and hoped that if I pulled the trigger something might happen.

I found a target when a rattle of pebbles came from the deeper darkness under the great stone, and I only just stopped myself in time from testing the gun. By then, in spite of the wind, I felt as if I were lying fully dressed in a sauna; fear is very good for the figure. The luminous face of my watch showed four minutes to midnight; I was, at least, on time, and the unknown under the stone could well be my informant. On the other hand it could be an enthusiastic Welsh owl watcher—or the garrotting expert. In my present state of mind I favoured the last, but someone had to make the first move.

'Good evening,' I said politely. 'Do you come here often?'

A scent of sandalwood, utterly alien to that bleak hill, drifted towards me. For one panic moment I remembered the killer's mark and my finger tightened on the trigger, then Vashni was against me sobbing.

'Darling, oh darling, thank God I've found you. Why are you here? Why did you leave me?'

I put my arms round her and the familiar feeling of safety welled gratefully into my mind. It was madness to doubt her, and if she were the killer I didn't care. Her voice steadied a little. 'I searched the house, and Larri hadn't seen you, then I went into Dawa's room to ask him and ...' Her body shuddered against me. 'Darling,' she said wildly, 'darling, I found something terrifying— and then I heard the cars and then you drove away.'

Her voice had risen to a frightened wail. I shook her and said sharply, 'All right what was it, tell me what it was.'

She drew a deep shuddering breath then asked quietly, 'Do you have a torch?'

I shielded the bulb and lit a small area of the pink stone between us. Her hand came into the pool of light holding a yellowing, postcard-sized photograph. It showed the head and shoulders of a man and had probably been taken for some official purpose since he was staring ahead with the living-dead expression of all passport photos the world over.

A white turban crowned a dark, rather cruel face. The features were strong and regular. A man in his middle years. A face I had seen very recently. Vashni's disembodied hand turned the card; on the back was a confusion of pothooks and dashes.

She read tonelessly, 'Sahiba, this is Chota's father, he died before you were born.'

I took it from her and examined the face. My mind was too full of her nearness to comprehend at first what I was seeing, then I whispered, 'Dawa! It's Dawa's face!'

There was no doubting it. Take away the disfigurement, the habitual foolish expression, and add a few years and it was unequivocably Dawa.

While I lay experiencing some very complicated emotions, Vashni was giving an excellent imitation of a leech. Her object was to get as large an area of body in contact with me as was possible under the existing laws of physics—and the sari didn't hinder her a bit. I picked up the torch and shone it full in her face. Short, straight nose, huge eyes innocent of anything but desire and love. Wide soft mouth quivering like an unhappy child. I lowered my head and kissed her, then laughed aloud.

She said, 'Darling. Oh dear, darling love, I was so frightened. You hated me; I didn't know where you were, but you hated me.'

I spent several minutes showing her she was wrong and I don't rate them as wasted time, but my mind churned steadily on with this new complication. Why had Dawa attached himself to Larri in disguise? He had only to turn up as Chota and he would have been welcome; true, if he wanted to be unrecognized something drastic would have had to be done, but in God's name what could be important enough to cause anyone to have such disfigurement deliberately inflicted?

How had he come by the photograph? I remembered his tiredness when he brought my breakfast that morning. By really moving he could have got to London, picked up Vashni's letter, and got back again in time not to be missed. The Bentley could have done it—but that kind of planning and action argued high intelligence, and training.

I sat up abruptly and Vashni made small protesting noises. I had known all along that there had to be a brain, other than Kommer's, behind it all. Now I was sure who owned it, and I had sent him off to smash his own organization—and Larri was with him. Then I remembered why I was there. In the excitement of finding Vashni, I had forgotten there should be a third person present. The cloud had settled down in a dark, hurrying mass; tendrils from its base brushed our faces and two paces away in the damp dark the great stone was invisible.

I hadn't much hope that our man had stayed through the reunion, but I took the torch and walked the forty-foot circumference of grey, chiselled rock. I left Vashni crouched at its foot, and, when the light picked out her blue sari again, I saw, pinned to the ground beside her, a scrap of white paper. Under it was a closely typed sheet of foolscap.

The paper carried one short Welsh sentence—'You do not come alone.'

The typescript was a list of names about a third of

which were ringed in red and ticked off in black ink. It was much the same as the one I had found in Kommer's desk, but the last name was entirely in red and there was no tick.

'Shivaro Larishnapur.'

Scrawled under it in Welsh: 'He now knows too much —they will kill him with the others tonight, after the landing at high tide.'

I translated for Vashni.

'When is high tide?' she asked calmly.

I made a rapid calculation. Ifor must have phoned about eleven-thirty.

'One-thirty.'

'What time is it now?'

Her voice was still calm and I wondered what kind of training could have given her such control. I had instinctively switched off the torch; it seemed like an arc light, exposing us unmercifully to whatever lay out there in the darkness. I looked again at the watch.

'Twelve-thirty.'

'Don't worry, darling,' she said. 'There's time enough, but I think we should hurry.'

We were back at the cars in ten minutes. I flung myself into the Lancia, set the ignition, and jammed the starter button. The engine heaved itself over but didn't fire. There was no time to play with it; I jumped out into the mud and called across to Vashni, 'There's something wrong, get yours going.'

When she didn't answer I ran forward shouting angrily, 'Get the damn thing going and back out!'

She appeared in the beam of the headlights. 'Darling,

the tyres ...' I shone the torch back at the Lancia's wheels
'... are slashed.'

'Yours too?'

She led the way to the small Ford standing at the end
of the yard. While we were on the hill someone had done
a really efficient job. Every tyre was in ribbons. I wasted
a few minutes trying to get some life into both engines—
a car will run on wheel rims if you're not worried about
its future; then I had the bonnets up and found both
rotor arms missing.

It was obvious how it had been done. Vashni was
followed; they wouldn't need lights if they kept close
enough to her. They'd had time to do the job comfortably and coast back down the hill in darkness. It would
have taken nerve, but whoever they were, they seemed
to have plenty of that.

'Time, darling?'

'Twelve-fifty.'

I had answered automatically, while desperately driving
my brain to recall details of the survey map in Pen-
Clawdd hall.

Vashni tugged gently at my arm. 'Darling, can we
do it?'

With an effort I brought the map into focus.

'Not by road. Larri was wrong, it's nearer seven miles
than five.'

She caught her breath. 'But Larri ...'

'All right,' I said. 'We're going over the mountain. It
can't be more than a mile and a half to the other road.
All we do is get up to the stone again and walk west;

we must hit it somewhere and with luck we should come out near Hywel's farm.'

I didn't tell her I had sent Larri to Jenkins. As soon as I was near her it became patently obvious that she could have nothing to do with the evil under Pen-Clawdd cliffs—but she carried the mark.

The first half-mile was easy. A sheep track led down into a shallow upland valley, more or less in the right direction. The ridge of the stone sheltered us, but we could hear the droning roar of the wind above our heads. Only one thing made progress possible through that invisible wilderness. When I decided to go to Jamaica I had changed my usual watch for the one I use for diving. Its face carries a complicated array of hands, dials, and a compass, and without it we would have wandered on the mountain until morning.

The path ended abruptly in a bog; we skirted it for several hundred yards, climbing steadily all the way; then the wind hit us like a club. Down in the valley we had not realized its gathering strength; on this ridge the insensate invisible force driving straight into our faces stopped us in our tracks. I pulled Vashni close to me and stumbled, bent double, through a maze of small thorn bushes, each one an instrument for the wind to use in the shrieking threnody around us.

The human will is a strange force. Larri was in appalling danger; both of us loved him, yet there came a point when we sat holding each other in the lee of an outcrop of rock, with the unspoken knowledge between us that we were finished. Vashni took my wrist and I could almost feel the despair flowing from her as she peered at the watch dial. One-thirty.

Under the loom of Pen-Clawdd cliff Kommer would be unloading his cargo. Even for the sub it would be a hazardous landing. The wind was from the south-west, it had only to shift a point or two and the rock infested shore would be a death trap. Perhaps he would not be able to land? I felt a surge of relief. Larri would be with Hywel and I had a great deal of confidence in the ability of that Welsh fox to smell danger. My unknown correspondent had given no indication as to how Larri was to be lured into the caves. He wasn't a fool to walk blindly into a trap, but Dawa was with him, trusted implicitly ... I forgot my aching, wind-searched muscles, pulled Vashni to her feet and clawed up the slope ahead, clinging to rank, wiry tufts of grass. On the summit I lifted my head and peered, eyes watering, into the wind. A few hundred feet below, Carnenoc's lights shone in the black roaring pit of the west road valley. When we burst into the farm kitchen it was empty.

I shouted, 'Hywel! Larri! Where are you?'

'Gone to the village.'

I walked over to the open door of the bedroom. From the voice I had expected an old woman; the face that looked up from the bed was marked and lined enough but still young—she had been very beautiful.

'Who was with him, Mrs Jenkins?' I asked gently.

'No one.'

'What was he going to do?'

The grey, pain-washed eyes stared contemptuously up at me.

'Attend chapel.'

I crossed to the bed and took her hand. The bones felt light as a bird's under the translucent skin. We had been speaking English, now I switched to Welsh.

'He is in danger.'

The hand tightened on mine.

'We are his friends; are you sure no one was with him?'

There was a long pause. 'You swear you are his friends?'

I nodded.

'His cousin Ifor came for him. Look under the bed.'

I lifted the beautiful Swansea bedcover and pulled out a green-painted ammunition box. In it was a complete detonator set, fuses, and, carefully packed in a large tea caddy, a pound or so of grey putty. The woman had turned her head painfully on the pillow.

'Plastic explosive,' she said. 'Enough there to lift me to Ynysdeullyn burial yard, bed and all. Save a lot of trouble that would.'

'Did they taken any with them?' My voice was urgent.

'Yes, that lot is spare.'

Hywel was a fox who knew how to stop an earth.

I pushed the box back. 'Is there anything you need, Mrs Jenkins?'

Her eyes travelled slowly up from my feet and locked on mine. Welsh eyes, fire banked deep in them.

'I am twenty-six,' she said. 'I have lain here three years. What kind of question is that, my man, to a woman with a broken back? Shut the door as you go.'

Somehow Dawa had tricked him, and Larri had never come here. Vashni was standing quietly in front of the cooking range.

'Stay here with Mrs Jenkins,' I said harshly. 'I'll be back in the morning.'

She bent her head. 'Yes, Lord.'

I was halfway to the village before I remembered I had spoken to her in Welsh.

I took the lower track. Generations of use had cut it six feet deep into the hillside. The transformation of Dawa from a shambling, kindly simpleton to the sharp and terrible intelligence that directed the whole evil operation, made me glad of the cover. The wind was dying; gusting through the mountains, driving the remnants of the storm before it to soak the inland valleys. By the time I emerged from the track a full moon was drenching the village meadows with light. I had one bad moment before I reached the single twisting street; hooves pounded behind me, I threw myself down on the silver-washed grass and watched, high above, a bunch of mountain ponies racing like an animated heraldic frieze, down the council road. They were the only living creatures I met. Ynysdeullyn was a dark, empty negative of its daytime self, but at the top of the street a light shone in the policeman's house; I was tempted to go there for help, then remembered the fiasco of the north beach—it would be a waste of time and Larri had very little of that left.

I swung on to the house track and dropped down in the shadow of the first big outcrop of rock to give my lungs some nourishment. I had run fast for over two miles, I was thirty-five and at the moment I was feeling every hour of it. There was no point in checking the house, but I did it. Knowing who Dawa was, made it a very interesting exercise, I put on no lights and slid through each room like a cat with a bad case of piles. The whole place was empty but it held that indefinable feeling of having been very recently occupied. I didn't want to go out to the caves; Vashni was safe, and at the moment so was I, and I very much wanted to keep things that way. I gave myself all the right sensible arguments —then set out towards the cliff edge.

Hywel only sheared a few years off my life when he rose up in front of me since I had half expected to find him there. He beckoned, then slid feet first into space. After a moment's hesitation I followed and found a two-foot-wide path dropping in perilous zigzags across the cliff-face. The wind had died completely or I would never have attempted it. At the bottom I sat down violently jarring my spine on the shingle. My legs had developed what the medical profession call jacitation—involuntary spasmodic movement; it took me some time to persuade them to obey me. Hywel waited until I climbed shakily to my feet, then put his finger to his lips and crept through the house-sized boulders to a point where the headland right-angled away to the north.

Two figures stood ten feet above the sea on a flat platform of rock. Behind them loomed the mouth of a sizeable cave, and, in the crook of their arms, lay highly efficient automatic rifles. They were so near that when one of them struck a match I recognized him as one of Kommer's crew. Hywel put a hand against my head and turned it seaward. At first I could see only the black shapes of half-drowned reefs, then a low symmetrical line of rock leapt into focus and resolved itself into the sub lying in deep water about a quarter of a mile off shore. We retreated to the foot of the path.

Hywel said, 'Sixty immigrants landed an hour ago, now inside with Kommer; no other crew but those on guard—rifles and sidearms.'

He'd had a lot of practice in passing exact information.

'Larri?' I asked.

'He went down the cliff with that servant of his just as I arrived.'

'Why in hell didn't you ...?'

'Stop him? How could I? I was a hundred yards away, if I'd shouted the guards would have been ready for them and picked them off on the path.'

'So he's in the cave?'

'There or in the sea, but I didn't hear a struggle.'

'You wouldn't,' I said bitterly, and told him about Dawa.

'*Dialach!*' he said. 'Complicated, isn't it?'

'I was at Carnenoc,' I said. 'Your wife told me Ifor was with you.'

He jerked his head at the path. 'Up above covering us —I've no wish to be trapped down here. What else did Gwennie tell you?'

'I looked under the bed.'

'Ah yes, and you found more than a chamber-pot?'

I thought of the woman in the bed. 'What happened?' I asked softly.

When he answered his voice was completely matter of fact. 'She is my second. You don't often get a second chance as good as that, Tomas—you might remember that. She came on a job with me. A television mast; we objected, see, to the excessive use of the English tongue. Can you swim?'

'I asked you what happened.'

'We dropped the mast,' he said harshly, 'and one of the stay wires whiplashed. I got her away and she told the hospital she'd turned the tractor over—then she made me go home and put it on its side in case the police checked. I asked can you swim?'

'Why?'

'We're going to blow that sub.'

Hywel had had a very thorough training in destruction. He had come out on a dangerous mission where he knew the opposition would be armed but he carried no gun himself—he was an explosives man. I wondered just how many expensive artefacts of our technological age he had reduced to untidy heaps of waste material. Some men build, others demolish, if they can't do it with explosives they use words. This one had started young and destruction got into his blood. Like killing, it's a difficult virus to eradicate. I have often wondered what basic antibiotic of decency protects the average man after a war. We take him from school, teach killing as a notable occupation, pin medals on him and praise his deadly work, then when that particular politician's blunder is over, we shove him abruptly back to normal trades. No one has bothered to compile statistics, yet I'd give good odds that not one in a million take up murder as a way of life.

The rest of the contents of Mrs Jenkins's box was cached under a nearby boulder. I held a torch while Hywel worked. In ten minutes he had a crude but effective mine sealed in a large biscuit tin and encased in stout black plastic. It was about on a level with a home-made petrol bomb—and no doubt just as effective.

After years of aqua diving the swim out to the ship was no problem for me. Hywel didn't enjoy it, but he was giving me fifteen years and had insisted on carrying his own baby. The mine was tied to his back with a length of light cord, and it was by this that we had somehow to attach it to the target. It was fused at forty-five minutes and when it went off the entire cast was going to be very busy. Kommer wouldn't hang about on shore, he'd want to get out to his ship or what remained of it, and he'd take his crew with him. We would then stroll into the cave and have only one expert garrotter to deal with—simple, but I thought again of the grim statistics for which I now knew Dawa to be responsible, and it wasn't only the sea cold that made me shudder.

Two hundred yards out and we were clear of the in-shore reefs. We were also clear of the headland and in full view of the ship and the cave guards. The moonlight was, by now, bright enough for me to read the trade mark of a firm of cattle food suppliers printed on the plastic of Hywel's deadly package. We were an hour after full tide. The ebb drifted us gently towards our objective, and I had only to make token movements to stay afloat, but I was very conscious of the guns ashore. My back felt ten feet wide and covered with luminous paint.

There was no watch on the ship. The men by the cave could have seen anything bigger than a rowboat two miles out. After the sea the smooth steel of the anchor chain seemed almost warm to my touch; I hauled myself clear of the water and reached a hand down to Hywel, then footsteps echoed from the conning tower. I twisted and dived, seal-like, in one movement; down and under the black prow into the shadow on the starboard side.

We floated in the calm lee of the sub face down. Every now and then I had to turn over to get some air, but what I saw sent me burrowing back down as if the chilling wetness had been warm fluffy blankets. The squat figure of Kommer's first lieutenant was draped comfortably over the bridge rail. He was enjoying a pipe and he made it last fifteen minutes by my watch. When he finally knocked it out and went below I was shuddering uncontrollably. The waters round our island home are not designed to support human life even in mid-June. Hywel appeared beside me, blowing like an elderly sea-lion, then we made one complete circuit of the ship and proved to our complete satisfaction that there could be no resting place for the mine on the entire hull. Just to make sure I dived between the great twin screws and examined their housing. It was an eerie feeling—one touch on the right switch just then would have churned me to mincemeat. When I surfaced I reached for the deck rail and pulled myself aboard. Hywel obviously thought I was mad but allowed himself to be hauled up beside me. I had remembered the cargo hatch. Most of its cover was flush with the deck but it had a central depression a foot deep crossed by several steel bars; for emergency opening, I suppose.

We got the tin jammed down between the bars and lashed it to them. I don't know how long it took; at the time a hundred and fifty years would have seemed a conservative estimate. We were working ten feet from the open conning tower, in full view of the men ashore, and with a minimum of six crew members just under our feet. When we slid back into the water I had forgotten I was cold.

We had regained the shadow of the reefs when I glanced up and saw something large outlined on the cliff top. It moved and the full silhouette of a horse and rider came into focus. A moment later the rider slid off and vanished; there was only one place he could be. We clung to slimy rock and watched him reappear on the cliff-face and move swiftly down. Once on the beach he made straight for the angle of the cliff. It could have been Ifor, but why the horse? We stayed put, the heavy ground swell monotonously lifting our faces into moonlight and dropping us back into shadow.

The guards had retreated into the cave. After peering cautiously round the rock face the waiting figure climbed swiftly to the platform; then the action speeded up. Kommer's men rushed out like spiders on a shaken web; the intruder was a very small man and stood no chance. There was a brief struggle and a single, truncated scream, then I forgot Hywel and thrashed madly for the beach. I had no use for caution now—it had, beyond any possible doubt, been Vashni's voice.

CHAPTER NINE

I was in the cave mouth by the time Hywel reached the edge of the platform. He launched himself at me in a long sliding tackle, and the moon broke into shining fragments spinning inside my skull. They re-formed six inches from my eyes; it seemed a curious phenomenon, but after a time I decided it was only Hywel's face and tried to go back to sleep; it wasn't easy since he was slapping me hard and unemotionally with the back of a large hairy hand until I rewarded him by sitting up and trying to hit back. While I was out cold he had dragged me back to the shelter of the headland and, somehow, pulled me into my clothes.

I humped to my feet and was reeling back towards the cave when his voice followed me wearily.

'Right. You do that, Tomas. Walk in and let them shoot you. Do your woman a lot of good that will.'

'But Dawa ...' I babbled. 'The bastard'll kill her like a kitten, he's ...'

Hywell was staring hungrily out over the moonlit water. 'Don't be a fool,' he said shortly. 'According to your story he's been in a position to do that for years; why should ...?'

A flame lit in my aching skull. 'Don't you see?' I cried. 'He was using them before, but now they know who he is, he *must* kill them!'

Strangely, my mental pictures of Vashni were overlaid by her brother—the faces shifted and changed but were always one.

Hywel glanced at his watch. 'All right,' he said. 'Give me ten minutes and I'll come with you. When that package blows they'll be a damned sight too busy to think of killing.'

I stared down at my watch and it was like gazing into white fire; the dial growing until it filled my world, my ears singing to the soundless whirl of invisible spinning wheels. Ten minutes passed, but I stayed crouched under that rock, hypnotized by the horror of time being hurled into eternity.

Hywel sighed, and got to his feet. 'The water must have got in,' he said flatly. 'I used a mechanical timer. Stupid, should have used acid. Come on.'

He headed for the path.

'All right,' I said wearily. 'You get out of this, you've done your best and it's not really your fight.'

'When this is finished,' he snapped over his shoulder, 'I'll flatten you for that. Now listen ...'

We picked Ifor up at the top of the path. Apparently Vashni had told him she was going down to meet Hywel and he'd let her pass. He had a car in the drive of the house and a boat manned by two taciturn fishermen waiting at the village quay. Second line of action—Hywel had learned his logistics in a good school. The fishermen shoved off and started their engine, Hywel turned and raced up the village street.

The hole from which the unfortunate Gupta had emerged was an inconspicuous affair ten feet above low-water mark in the northern cliff—if he had got through the headland so could we and, if we moved fast, we might just hold things up long enough for Hywel to gather the village. The only way I could keep going was to think of the whole problem as a poker game—action and bluff, bluff ... and action ... The cave stank. A musty creeping odour, hard to define, but it could well have originated in the piled up debris of ancient crab pots in one corner. Thirty feet back, air whistled down a vertical shaft; there was no other exit.

I climbed first; Ifor followed, cursing steadily. The whole thing funnelled in towards the top and gave me a bad moment in that draughty blackness when I thought we might not be able to pass, then I was through and emerged on to dry, smooth stone. I chanced one quick flash of the torch beam, then left it on, swinging steadily across the walls of a cave that would comfortably have housed two football pitches. At various levels, from the sixty-foot-high ceiling to the smooth honey-coloured floor, the mouths of innumerable tunnels pockmarked the walls. The ancient Celts had known what they were doing when they christened the headland—we were deep in the anthill.

Looked at from the calm into which I had bludgeoned my reeling mind, there was nothing wrong with the cave. Claustrophobia is a neurosis that has never bothered me. Whenever a subway train performs its usual trick of sliding to a halt in its burrow, and deep earth-heavy silence flows over the lines of helpless commuters, I can watch with amused compassion the small signs of carefully hidden fear that shadow their respectable faces, but this hole in the ground held something different. It was a place I very much wanted to get away from. A nebulous creeping horror hung in the air like spiritual fire-damp and, oddly enough, the musty smell of the entrance seemed to have followed us and intensified. I swung the torch beam methodically over the holes on the far wall. We had to make a choice and make it quickly and, if it were a mistaken one, we could wander for hours through the heart of the rock, losing forever the slim remaining chance of saving Vashni and her brother. I forced myself to think clearly. Gupta had come that way. He had no broken bones when I met him, so I eliminated any entrance above ten feet from the cave floor; many of the remainder were obviously impassable. Many were too low for a frantic man to have run through at his full height. This narrowed the choice to eight. My control was slipping; I wanted to throw myself frantically into any one of those black mouths, crying aloud for Vashni.

I waited while Ifor reduced the odds by proving three tunnels as dead ends; he was away for ten minutes in one of them, and by the time he returned, I was reduced to near madness by anxiety and the increasing psychic pressure of that vile place. We made the final choice by striking matches and watching for the strongest current of air to disturb the flame. As we entered Ifor asked, 'Do you smell anything?'

'The whole place stinks,' I answered irritably.

'Yes, but it's at its worst in here, man.'

He set off at a lope down the passage, the broad torch beam flooding the floor ahead.

Our pace quickened imperceptibly until we were running hard, swaying and panting, clawing the filthy air into labouring lungs; then Ifor switched off the torch and stopped in his tracks, I crashed into him and we ended in a tangled heap; the taste of his fish-grimed hand clamped over my mouth momentarily blotting out the all pervading, sickly sweet smell. Ahead, a faint glow flickered on the walls of the passage.

Up to now I had been concerned only with getting to Vashni, and I had no coherent plan except that I was quite prepared to kill anyone who got in my way, but to do that I would have to get within hand distance of them. Our weaponry was not sophisticated; between us we had the torch and Ifor's fishing knife.

We inched forward keeping as flat as possible. It wasn't a happy method of progression; at floor level the air was unbreathable—heavy with a savage, putrefying stench that knotted the stomach as reluctant lungs dragged it in. I had thought the light to be a reflection dimmed by distance, but ten yards from where we had fallen we found the source and the floor ceased to exist.

My reaction to what was below was curious. One half of my mind seemed coldly to assess the data and pass it to another for comment; the more details of the scene that unfolded the more this mental dichotomy increased. Perhaps, just as there is a physical threshold of pain beyond which the nervous system refuses to operate, there may be a mental barrier against horror ...

The passage was split by a shaft some ten feet across. From where I lay, I could see that it spread out some way below and became the ceiling of a lower cave of indeterminable size. It was not possible to assess the size of the cave because of that which was heaped high above its floor. Beside me I heard Ifor vomit.

A pyramid of naked human bodies, its apex reaching high into the shaft, spread down to the floor of the lower level. A festering heap rising from loathsome ambiguous corruption through every gradation of decay to a group of new-comers pathetic and perfect in death, so close below me I could have touched the outstretched hand of the nearest. The horror that broke the unnatural calm of my mind was realization of the source of light. The heap *glowed* with a flickering cold blue flame. The decay, I suppose, caused it but the effect was to make those nameless things seem to stir and live.

I had thought that nothing could tear my mind from Vashni, but I stayed on my knees in that strange place until the horror became a norm, and the brown face of the topmost body seemed that of an old friend. As if from a great distance I heard Ifor shout, 'Watch it!' Then his shoulder crashed against me and I rolled sideways and down on to the sprawled body beneath.

From where I lay Kommer looked gigantic, almost filling the passage on the far side of the pit. The corpse light had vanished and his grotesque face was lit by the prosaic glare of naked electric lamps hanging from the rock ceiling. The gun in his right hand lifted steadily towards me. There was no point in moving. I felt comfortable and at peace. The dead brown man beneath me was my friend and soon we would sink together into the amorphous comradeship of the pile under us. I felt consciousness ebb as the fumes from the cave took hold.

Kommer knelt, reached down a hand, and heaved me

to the rock floor beside him.

I closed my eyes and muttered thickly, 'Finish it, you bastard.'

The familiar roar of his laugh boomed through the passage and echoed uneasily from the cave of the bodies.

'You are too rare a jewel to throw on a muck heap,' he said. 'The only man who ever stood up to me.' He held out a hand. 'Come, my friend.'

Something flashed from the darkness on the far side of the pit. Kommer grunted, dropped the gun and clutched at his groin. He stared down reproachfully at me, then rolled slowly, almost gracefully, forward, just missing the apex of the pile and I heard one of the most unpleasant sounds of my life as he struck the slope further down. I picked up the torch and focused it on him. He was in that dreadful heap to his armpits. I called his name and he twisted convulsively sinking to his neck. He spoke in German, then threw back his head and said calmly in English,

'Traherne, use my gun; shoot me quickly. I should not die this way.'

Ifor leapt the pit and dropped beside me neatly as a cat. He straightened up, with Kommer's huge gun swinging idly in his hand, and stared down the slope of the foetid pyramid.

'Drown, you bastard,' he said sweetly. 'Why should we help you?'

A small sucking voice came from below—the sound of a baby at the breast. Kommer screamed once. I waited for the echo to die before looking down. The head was tipped back, and only the bladderlike face swam now on the viscous surface. Instinctively I dropped on my knees and reached down. As I touched it the topmost corpse turned towards me, shifted by the struggle below. The dead eyes seemed faintly amused.

I got slowly to my feet; this horror was of Kommer's making. With grotesque accuracy the law of cause and effect was operating before my eyes. This man was personally responsible for every molecule of the filth that was eating him; who was I to stand between him and the manner of his death?

I remembered then that, in his own fashion, he had liked me, and, even with the dreadful evidence of what he had done bubbling round him, I could not hate him. It came to me then that perhaps there is no such thing as hate—only the dark side of love—and that is something to which I still cling.

He screamed again then moaned, 'Kill me! Ah, kill me!'

I reached a trembling hand towards the gun, but Ifor clamped it in an iron grip.

'Die, you murdering sod!' he snarled, and lifted the long barrel.

I waited for the shot, but in one swift movement he tossed the gun deliberately down into the upturned face.

Kommer screamed, *'Mütter!'* The rose-bud lips pouted above the surface for one long moment, then the slime moved sluggishly and he was gone.

'Bloody shame losing my knife,' Ifor said. 'Had her for years.'

A hundred yards along the passage we found a door. It was built of three-inch-thick steel plate and had probably been designed for a bank vault. The massive hinges were set deep in the rock. If Kommer hadn't opened it our trip would have finished there, but, beyond, we found a flight of concrete steps leading up to a landing and a normal wooden door. It was a very ordinary place. We started up the steps, then I went back and closed the door to the corridor of the pit.

I never found out much about Ifor's background but at some time in his life he'd had some basic urban guerrilla training. He slammed the wooden door open with one foot, jumped through and pitched flat. I followed him more sedately. I don't know what I had expected to find, but after the pit it was like waking from a nightmare. We were in a small, beautifully furnished room. The carpet was made of some kind of black fur, so thick it was difficult to realize naked rock lay under it. The walls were hung with heavy black velvet. An elegant Louis XV bureau filled most of one wall with matching chairs on either side. Opposite, a fake fireplace of the same period completed the drawing-room illusion. Above the mantelpiece a small, very ancient, black statuette with eight arms was set in a crystal frame. Larri and Vashni sat at either end of a large sofa. The only discordant note was struck by Dawa standing immobile against a door opposite and holding a rifle very ready for any move any of us might decide to make. Ifor climbed to his feet and held up his hands. He was evidently too old a campaigner to try heroics.

'Come in, Tomas,' Larri said languidly. 'We were getting just a little anxious about you.'

I couldn't take my eyes from Vashni. She sat poised

and elegantly beautiful; except for the sari I was reminded of when she had first come into my office. I felt a rush of gratitude that it was possible to love another human being so much and started towards her ignoring the menacing rifle. She held both arms out to me; I knelt beside her keeping my eyes carefully away from Dawa and spoke rapidly in bad French hoping he would not understand.

'Thank God you're both safe. Kommer's dead but that bastard behind you has been king pin all along. Larri, try and fool him. See if you can get him out into the room where we can jump him.'

Larri nodded imperceptibly, turned his head and snapped a curt sentence in Urdu.

I said loudly, 'Ifor, when I shout "go" jump the sod.' I spoke in Welsh.

'Right,' Ifor said. 'Got it. Proper little United Nations aren't we?'

I turned towards him and saw his face change. Behind me Vashni screamed, then something took me round the throat. Larri's voice came smoothly in my ear.

'I don't want to kill you, Tomas, so don't give me trouble,' then to Ifor: 'If you move he's dead.'

CHAPTER TEN

Dawa crossed the room and shoved one of the Louis XV chairs against the back of my knees. I collapsed into it and the band round my throat relaxed, but I knew better than to struggle—I'd been through this one before. When I turned my head fractionally the great hawk ring that I had last seen with Gupta, glowed on Larri's right hand.

'The family emblem,' he said cheerfully. 'We all carry it one way or another; they mark our women at birth.'

Well, that cleared up one mystery.

Dawa crossed to the fireplace, put the rifle carefully down beside him, and bowed to the idol.

I lifted my eyes to the eight-armed Goddess. 'How could you?' I wondered aloud. 'You of all people.'

Larri waved a negligent hand. 'No trouble at all, my dear fellow—just tradition. I was dedicated when I was ten and gave her my first sacrifice when I was twelve. The males of the family have been her priests and protectors of her servants for two thousand years. Now Vashni, of course, is Dûrga—the other side of the coin, you see.'

'No I don't see,' I said furiously. 'It's bloody absurd, no one can ...'

'You don't believe a family could last so long? Well Larishnapur's not Westminster you know.' He smiled slightly. 'Perhaps the dry air preserves the family tree.'

It was fantastic. My mind fought against the knowledge, but beyond all doubt he was responsible for that obscene holocaust behind the steel door, yet he exuded the same charming gaiety as always. His hands moved restlessly at my neck.

'I had hoped you would live up to your reputation. Why on earth didn't you get away safely with Vashni when I gave you the chance? Was she such a small prize for me to offer?' His voice changed to anger. 'Damn it! Why do you think I even permitted you near her? When Dawa stopped me killing you at the river he explained what enormous use you could be. I must say I hadn't thought of it, but it would have worked out perfectly. There was only the barrier of your birth, but I had my suspicions about that and I was right. We had your family traced back for six hundred years, it was most interesting; your line is princely so it was no dishonour if you had Vashni, and through her I could control you in a far more efficient manner than Kommer with his crude blackmail.'

I hadn't the faintest idea how he had managed to trace my family—it was more than I'd ever been able to do; and the whole thing was, of course, absurd. If you go back far enough any Welshman is a prince. Yet he wasn't mad, not in any ordinary sense.

I forgot the thong round my neck and exclaimed angrily, 'Why? Why do it? You were handed everything you could want in a golden bloody spoon. You've got the lot and yet you take up a dirty murderous trade and try to justify it with some damned voodoo ritual. What happened? Did you run out of kicks?'

He seemed genuinely surprised. 'My dear fellow, for

the money of course. I leave the—ah—voodoo to Dawa. I am, I fear, a sybarite with very expensive tastes. Nowadays the hereditary revenue drops with a hollow thud into the sticky hands of Government babus in Delhi, and the pension I'm supposed to live on wouldn't keep me in shoes. Do you realize I make over a million a year?' He chuckled. 'Tax free, of course.'

He could have been an organization man discussing salary; but while he spoke his eyes turned uneasily towards the squat figure of the Goddess.

'But why kill?' I persisted. 'Surely the poor bastards pay enough?'

'Tradition again,' he said gaily. 'One mustn't interfere with one's manager, and friend Dawa is a stickler for tradition. The Sect has always killed. The sacrifice must be made, and it might as well be profitable. Our visitors know it. As soon as they walk in here and see *her* ...' He jerked his chin at the idol. 'They give up. Your friend Gupta was an exception, he panicked before we put on the lights; normally we have very little trouble with them.'

'Larri,' I said, 'take that damned washing line away from my neck and come round where I can see you.'

There was a long silence, and for one endless moment the thong tightened. Vashni started forward like a tigress, hands crooked towards her brother; Dawa thrust her casually back into her seat, and, behind me, Larri laughed. I must have closed my eyes. When I looked again he stood before me, poised and graceful. Looped over his hands was a long red cord, the ends frayed into small gilded tufts. He smiled down at me and there was not a hint of evil in the twinkling black eyes. I had loved him because he was part of Vashni, and liked him because of his quite genuine charity work for the immigrants. How complex could a mind be? Was it possible to house good, and incredible evil in one body? He had the same uncanny trick as his sister, and answered as though he had read my thoughts.

'You could never understand me. Your mistake is thinking of us as European, but Vashni and I belong to something older than you cream-faced children can imagine. What can you know of Reality, with your minds cut into neat compartments? I tell you there are levels of awareness that you people can't dream of; levels where opposites meet; levels where good is evil, black is white, light is darkness, and only Perfection is seen.' His voice rose. 'How can you know of the ecstasy of Death—the sacred bond between killer and killed?'

He moved restlessly over to face the Goddess, keeping carefully out of Dawa's line of fire.

I looked at Vashni and she seemed to exist in a dream. Her eyes were fixed unwaveringly on me.

'Larri ...' I said hoarsely, 'Larri, she ...'

'Knew nothing.' He spoke as though soothing a child. 'I told you she serves Dûrga.'

Every sweat pore on my body opened as I relaxed away from the weight of fear that had lain on me since I saw the emblem on her thigh. At that moment I found I couldn't hate him. Those in the pit must take their own revenge; now I had to keep him occupied until Hywel arrived—or was beaten to it by the rest of Kommer's crew. My mind raced.

'Look,' I said, 'can't we make a deal? If I have Vashni I can't very well ...' My voice trailed away under his amused gaze.

'No,' he said gently. 'I admit I haven't liked anyone so much for years. I really *am* fond of you, but whatever I gave you now—even Vashni—you'd betray me. You've too much damned Welsh non-conformist conscience to work with me. I decided that yesterday and that's why I brought you here tonight.'

'Brought me?'

He laughed. 'Yes, of course. *I* wrote the last message. I've no more idea than you who your pen pal is, but it was easy enough to fake that infantile writing, and Vashni and I have studied Welsh for months.' He chuckled again, a high-spirited man delighting in a ruse to fool his friend. 'I left the list too. Kommer told me you'd searched his cabin and seen one like it, in fact he planted Chota's name on that one especially for you, and that gave me the idea. I knew you'd come rushing off the mountain to the rescue—and I made sure it would take you long enough for me to get tonight's cargo ashore before I dealt with you.' The cord moved in his hands like a live red snake. 'But it was inconsiderate of you to use the tradesman's entrance; you were supposed to be picked up at the front by Kommer's men.'

Something was wrong. There was a piece of the puzzle missing, a vitally important piece. I scrabbled through my brain for the answer. Keep him talking!

'You couldn't have written it,' I said slowly. 'There was another message at the standing stone; it said, "You do not come alone." How the devil could you have known

Vashni would follow me?'

From in front of the idol Dawa spoke, 'How could you have known that, Lord?'

Larri padded over towards him. 'Because I sent her,' he said.

Dawa cried, 'Fool!' and rose, towering above his master. 'Oh, my Lord, you were foolish, now she can betray us, she ...'

The sweat had dried on me. I shivered, but was stiflingly aware of the room as an isolated bubble of gas in the matrix of the earth, a million tons of rock bearing down above us.

Through the utter silence Larri said. 'She will not betray us.'

I was moving as he spoke, but Ifor hurtled past me before I was half way out of the chair. Vashni screamed once, but the sound died as it was born, choked back into her lungs. We froze where we stood. A strand of scarlet circled her throat, the lithe body arched back over the sofa —a human bow bent by the deadly archer behind her.

I heard myself screaming, 'Leave her; ah, Christ! Don't kill her.'

His gaiety had gone, breath rasped into his lungs like an animal in distress. I was on my knees; arms held imploringly towards him, hands making small, useless, pleading movements. He shook his head as though some dreadful net enclosed it, and screamed at the small, placid Goddess, 'I won't do it! I won't! I won't!'

Saliva hung in loops from his mouth. His whole body shuddered, jerked and writhed. A man fighting for his life, but fighting an invisible enemy. Quite dreadfully the

183

struggle ceased at his wrists. The hands, with a horrid life of their own, calmly and inexorably tightened the cord.

He screamed again, 'Krishna! Ai, Krishna!' and something sprang from Dawa's hand. The killing cloth wrapped over the bulging eyes.

Then I found myself lying on him, my hands at his throat, his heels drumming soundlessly on the fur of the carpet. I had forgotten who I was. It was enough to kill, to feel life ebbing under my hands. Joy leapt and surged in my blood; a pleasure greater than any I had known, leading inevitably towards an unthinkable orgasm of the spirit. When Ifor hauled me away, I fought him. I could hear an animal snarling and an odd observant corner of my mind realized it was myself.

Vashni's face formed dreamlike through a scarlet veil. I fell forward into her arms, something unspeakable slipped out of my mind, and its going was a trauma greater than birth; then, with my full weight on her she stood erect, facing the Thing above the fireplace, singing three words over and over; a thin, clear, nasal sound.

Dawa was on his knees beneath the image, the rifle forgotten beside him, the ravaged face heavy with sadness.

'Kali chose you,' he said. 'She chose you and you let Her go.'

From far away I heard shots and confused shouting. Footsteps pounded towards the door, a rifle butt splintered the lock. A dozen fishermen raced into the room, faces blackened, modern army-pattern rifles in their hands. Hywel strolled in after them and looked down at Dawa.

'Chapel meeting is it?' he said. 'Come on, out of it all of you.'

Larri stumbled forward, a rifle barrel jammed in the small of his back, but he seemed utterly harmless. His intense vitality had drained from him leaving the face slack and empty. The outer cave was crowded with the sub's last cargo, frightened brown faces shrinking back from the armed men. At the sea entrance, we pushed aside black plastic curtains and passed from the yellow glare of electricity to white, cold moonlight. Two of Kommer's crew lay sprawled on the rock, and, out beyond the reefs, I could just distinguish the dark outline of the waiting sub.

Vashni pressed hard against me, kissing my face and hands while the fishermen looked carefully away. I was concerned only to get her clear of the whole deadly mess. She was a strong-minded woman but she had been through quite enough, and there was, in any case, our future to think of. It would be as well if, by tomorrow, we were on a Jamaica-bound plane. When the police and the media got hold of this lot, anyone connected with it would stink. I'd have to rely on Hywel and the village to meet Lettcombe with blank Welsh incomprehension. She lifted her face, eyes glittering in the moonlight.

'Are you safe?' she asked. 'Are you really safe?'

'Of course I am,' I said gently. 'We both are. Come on, *cariad*, time we went.'

She moved a pace away. 'You will not kill. You must never kill.'

'Now look,' I said sharply, 'what's all this about?'

'Kali,' she whispered. 'For a moment she took you. I

drove her out, but I could do it only because you love me. Usually when she takes a man, nothing can make him leave her; and now you can never leave me. I will guard you—life after life ...'

She took my hands and pressed them to her breasts until I felt the nipples harden under my palms.

I swallowed and said lightly, 'Well come on, love, never mind the next life, let's get on with this one.'

One of Kommer's men groaned and tried to turn over. She left me at once and crossed to him.

'He's alive,' she said crisply. 'He must have help.'

'There's nothing more you can do here,' Hywel called urgently. 'I'll see to him. Now get going, and when the police come I've never heard of you. Go on, get out of this, I've got to get these guns hidden.'

No more can be required, surely, of any one than the best he can do at a given moment? I don't think I could have done more, but I must live now, always, with that question; and with something else within me. An oddly shaped shadow glimpsed at the limit of inner vision—a patch of darkness in the cellars of my mind.

We had all forgotten Larri. No one could know what dark change had come to his mind in those few appalling moments in front of the Goddess, but the spark was gone. The muttering, slack-jawed creature crouched in the cave mouth seemed as harmless as a village idiot. I turned away, calling impatiently for Vashni. A blur of movement caught my eye, and I swung back towards her, then stopped in my tracks.

Larri's empty eyes were alive again, but it was not he

who looked out. The thin face was changed beyond recognition. For a moment he stood, towering above his sister as she knelt beside the wounded man, then the scarlet cord flowed through his hands like a jet of blood, etching itself vividly against the pallor of her throat. I shrieked once, and was beside her, scooping her into my arms as she toppled forward. The whole thing took, perhaps, three seconds.

I turned towards Larri, crouching now under the guns of the village people. No one spoke, then Hywel put a rifle on a ledge beside me and walked with his men back into the cave.

The snap of the bolt as I rammed home a shell echoed back from the cave. Larri squatted on his haunches. His face, emptied again and remote, was the face of the dead Vashni. Beside me, Dawa rose from the shadows and stood erect, his killing cloth held on upturned palms; in the ruined face the dignity of a priest. Under the bright stare of his eyes my hands trembled and I lowered the gun. His calm gaze moved to Vashni's face.

'I would have saved her,' he said. 'She, a Great One, cared when she thought me lost: she cared knowing I was casteless dirt. But the Goddess knows Her own needs.'

He nodded down towards Larri. 'He took me as a boy and taught me the mysteries. Whatever he required, I did. When there was need, I killed. When he ordered, I destroyed even my own face.'

I stared at him. Any resemblance to a child's toy had gone. To carve one's own face into that grotesque mask was unthinkable, yet he had done it, and sad eyes stared

187

back from the remnants of what must have been noble beauty.

'Why?' My voice was a whisper of sound just audible above the sea wash on the rocks below.

He shrugged. 'I had a birthmark—a white crescent across one cheek. As a child, other children teased me saying it was a Moslem mark. But it is also one of Kali's signs for Her chosen.'

'Then why destroy it?'

'Because he wished it. I was suspected in our district; people had vanished when I had been near them. Here, no one was to know me. Chota Dal was to die—I was now Dawa Chand. A new man in a new country, free to do his bidding.'

A small wind stirred the hair of my dead self beside me. I stroked it from her face, and Dawa followed the movement with his eyes.

'She and my Lord are one,' he said. 'She is Dakshina-cara, the bright path, that which colours the darkness. He, Vamacara, the darkness itself. One cannot exist without the other.'

He pointed with his chin at the man crouched on the rock. 'Greed destroyed him. I did the work in purity—he for money and power. All my life, in our own country, I trusted and loved him, but Kali knew and, at last, when we came here, She showed me my path. I wrote the letters ...'

'But they were in Welsh.'

'What of it? I know ten languages of Hind—what was one more?' His voice held an edge of impatience, a teacher interrupted in his thesis. 'When the Lady Vasentasena came to you in her search for me as Chota Dal, my Lord marked you for killing, but I knew you had power and could destroy him for me. Therefore Kali protected you from the lorry, and I saved you beside the river.'

'Why not kill him yourself?'

'If *you* had destroyed him I could have continued unknown and alone, working only for the Dark One.' His voice dropped, and he made a curious gesture towards his master. 'And now he is finished, for *She* has taken his mind to eat in darkness ...'

I looked at Vashni. The sari clung to her, revealing the swelling beauty of her breasts, the tender line of the thighs. For the first time I understood my loss. Grief churned my guts. Anger beat at the walls of my skull; I swung the rifle up and fired. A line of blood, black in the moonlight, appeared across the back of Dawa's hand. When the echoes died he looked wonderingly at me and asked, 'Did your Lady teach you nothing?'

I thought of what she had taught me and put my head in my hands and wept.

'Why sorrow?' he asked curiously. 'You will be with her now to the end of this Kalpa—a thousand thousand years. Why kill me? I could have killed you many times, but you were no sacrifice. If I killed, you would be reborn; a snake under my feet, a disease in my blood, a child growing towards my destruction. May I go now?'

Someone with my voice said, 'Go in peace.'

He bent down and lifted Larri to his feet, taking the red killing cord from his hands.

'Come, Lord,' he said gently. 'It is time to go.'

An Aldis lamp stuttered urgently from the waiting

sub as Hywel ran from the cave and snatched up the rifle.

'*Dialch!*' he snapped. 'What kind of a man are you? You're letting the bastards get away.'

I knocked the barrel aside, a shot whined angrily along the cliff-face and, below us, a boat's engine coughed twice and burst into life. Dawa certainly knew how to handle it. In two minutes it must have been doing thirty knots.

The villagers and immigrants crowded out of the cave together, then, as we watched, the engine note changed and the launch swung wildly off course. On its deck two figures met, parted, and met again—dancers moving with eerie precision through the steps of a deadly ballet. For a moment the outlines of the launch and the submarine merged, then the sea boiled in the moonlight, the beat of giant diesels mingled with the scream of a klaxon and the long, black shape of the sub wavered and vanished under the water. Uneasy echoes muttered in the honey-combe of the cliff.

Out on the bay the launch turned blindly in widening circles, when it passed through the moonpath a single figure could be seen slumped across the stern. I became aware of Hywel shaking me violently.

'Which one got away?' he cried. 'Which of the sods got away?' Some far away corner of my mind was amused that, under stress, he spoke English.

I said wearily, 'Does it matter?' and stooped to pick up my dead.

They tried to take her from me, but I climbed the track with her in my arms; I was still holding her when the last man appeared over the cliff edge. Hywel shouted orders and the crowd streamed over the headland towards the house, the Welsh pulling off their woollen hats as they passed, the Indians making full *namasti*, pressing their foreheads into the grass.

I stared out along the moonpath. I had only to turn into the silver wash of light and I would see her face. Would her eyes be open? Still full of that amused secretiveness that women keep for their personal man? I buried my face in her hair. Freed from its silver ring it fell, a sandalwood-scented column of darkness, melting into the deep darkness at my feet. My arms tightened round her. With her I was home, warm and safe. Why go out again into the cold?

An intolerable light glared through the curtain of her hair, piercing my shut eyelids, waking me from the warm dream. Far out a tree of fire had grown from the sea. It towered, blossomed, and died.

Hywel spoke from behind me. 'There's mistiming for you. Getting old I am.'

The house was full of a bizarre collection of villagers, policemen and immigrants. They made way for me as I carried Vashni upstairs to my room. I was very glad when I could lay her on the bed; I had not believed it possible to be so tired and still remain upright. I sank down beside her, remembering what Dawa had said, and what she had tried to tell me outside the cave. We would be together again. Maybe she was right, but what in hell use was that to me? I needed her now. I climbed wearily to my feet, then bent and kissed her eyes and each corner of the quiet mouth.

I took the stairs very slowly, and with great care, counting them as I went. When I reached thirty I found I was in the hall, and felt, with quiet satisfaction, that I had achieved something. I lifted my head and I was standing on a vast chequered plain. Somewhere across it was a way of escape. I moved slowly forward, counting the black and white tiles, placing each foot meticulously in their centres. After the twentieth tile I looked up and a silver sea path stretched away below, curving over the edge of the world. The door was open. I walked through it—no one tried to stop me.

Away from the tiles there was nothing to count. I felt turf and rock turn and spin beneath my feet. On hands and knees I clawed my way forward, and saw, thankfully, that the path was still there far below. One more effort and I would be safely on it. Someone seized me and hauled me to my feet.

'Come along, sir.' Lettcombe's voice was very gentle. 'I'm taking you home.'